To Little Mother
who never forget
My Birthday

Jack Webb

From Where The Sun Stands Now, Then Forever Stands

by

Jack F. Reich

authorHOUSE™

1663 LIBERTY DRIVE, SUITE 200
BLOOMINGTON, INDIANA 47403
(800) 839-8640
WWW.AUTHORHOUSE.COM

First published by AuthorHouse 07/06/05

ISBN: 1-4208-5892-0 (sc)
ISBN: 1-4208-5893-9 (dj)

Library of Congress Control Number: 2005904539

Printed in the United States of America
Bloomington, Indiana

This book is printed on acid-free paper.

Introduction and Author's Notes

I have created a near perfect environment for a she wolf and her pups, also at the same time I incorporated a band of Sioux Indians and their daily lives, to live in close parallel with the wolf family. As the book unfolds, the wolf pack becomes the scouts for the Sioux, joined by eagle, which was helped by the she wolf, and is repaying the she wolf for the favor. At this time I must in form you dear reader the book is a fantasy, pure fiction and is before white man had a chance to influence the open splendor of the vast prairies, so no place in this book is he, or any of his ways mentioned the closeness between wolf and Indians came about in a raging spring snow storm were Moon Boy almost blind sun of the band chief Tall Elk, would have perished, had not the wolves stepped in and saved the boy. At this time, it was discovered that he could speak with the wolves, and they to him but that was the only way it worked. Moon Boy and the pack could freely speak to other animals, but all else had to be translated by Moon Boy just six summers old.

Some violence, as our Sioux have to defend them selves, from other war like braves raiding for horses and girls or anything worth stealing, not bad just the way it was done in those days. Tall Elk was lucky for he had ground and air surveillance, so no one could ever sneak up on him. Now there were eight wolves and three eagles scouting twenty four seven.

Jack F. Reich

Chapter One

The time was middle February. It was a cold, blustery evening and the light evening breeze was moving snow over the land. The upper slopes of the Moreau River country were bleak and barren; it had been a slow growing year. Sparse patches and bunched grass stopped the snow from going on south east across the river. The she wolf was nervous, ever now and again turning to look at her enlarged belly, whimpering to herself only to run on looking for a better place to den. She moved up through a plum patch that grew up against an overhang where water and wind had formed a deep cut. At one end a large rock had tipped over, forming a snug depression. Grass and weeds had almost covered the mouth of the opening and the she wolf slid low to peer inside the opening. The floor was littered with tumble weeds and leaves. The she wolf slid inside turned around one way and then the other gave a contented grunt and lay down. She had found what she had looked for all day.

Curly found himself in a dark world. He was up against something warm and he wiggled his nose from side to side. He found a projection, and out came his little pink tongue which found a drop of something sweet and good: he opened his mouth and drank. Then he was aware of a new sensation, a something warm and wet was smoothing down his fur; it began from his nose all the way back to his tail and it felt so nice. He was sleepy, warm and full. Curly was dozing when he was startled back to awareness. He was not alone, there were other small wiggling forms near him making squawking gurgling grunting sounds, and that was not all.

The sounds were all different; at least five or six other little bodies were close to him. He took a full breath of air and discovered something else; they all had a distinct, separate odor. The big one who was so warm and kind and gave him food smelled like milk. The other small wiggling things smelled like milk also but different; each one of them had an odor different from all the rest and the one next to him had a musky odor. His grunt was deep and full and when he moved close to Curly, he had power; his name was Cubby. He was Curly's full brother and would be his lifelong companion. Then there was a little sister Sniff. She was small and quick and she smelled like wind in the far away.

Her voice was soft when she moved against Cubby, her raspy growl, no more then a whisper, but she was there and they all knew it. Fatty was next, irritable, grumpy, and short tempered. Even as little as Fatty was, he wanted to be tough, and he smelled like wind just passed. He moved to his left and bumped Sniff, trying to get her food. She was small but strong and held on. Fatty turned to his right and found Ling Lang. He was mild in nature and smelled like dusty rain. When Fatty pushed him he got a hold of Fatty's ear in his mouth and bit as hard as he could.

The startled yelp disturbed the mother who had been dozing after her labor of the past twelve hours. She observed her pups, caressing them with her tongue and gathering them to her, keeping them warm. The last of the litter was another litter sister, Dusty Rose. She had come last, small and a little frail but strong enough. She was kind and cuddly and she was half under Ling Lang, staying warm and eating beside her brother. She smelled like grass after a summer rain.

The mother wolf was pleased. Surviving was hard and there had been that time in mid November when the food supply had almost disappeared. All she could find was a few half-starved grasshoppers to eat. No rain meant the water holes were gone and with them, gone there would be no frogs, snakes, or salamanders if one looked hard you may find a dried up fish or two. Late December was hard, for she was alone and carrying her litter. She had covered long miles in those days only stopping to rest when necessity demanded.

One late evening she came to an abandoned camp. The Sioux had broken camp that morning, leaving little in passing, as they were hungry too. Hunting was bad on the high plains and river bottoms, and the game had moved on to find grass. She smelled the camp before she came up to it; there were the usual things left behind, worn out foot ware, cast off clothing, and then she remembered the fire pits. The pits were cool now so she approached the first one in large circle of rocks, possibly a head mans lodge. The pit was large and fairly deep.

She begun to dig almost at once, and she was rewarded in finding a scrap of meat, badly burnt but edible. She did not mind the charcoal taste, and ate greedily. Next, a bone was uncovered that had meat fat and gristle still attached. By dark she had eaten her fill and even found another bone for chewing. The next morning she was gone and by first light flushed out a grouse with a broken wing; this was the first good meal in along time. Ten miles more in a brushy draw a buffalo bull had broken a leg in a bad fall, and so she stayed a week or until there was not much left. By now the wolf had gained some strength and a much needed rest. January was a hit and miss time and so was February and now that the pups were here it was time to hunt again.

Curly became aware that something was not as it should be, something was different, and he looked for the projection which was not where he left it. He was beginning to get a little hungry, and now a little upset. Were had he put his projection? It fit on the big warm something that was so nice and made his fur smooth. He would move up, find his mother, and then every thing would be just fine. He wiggled up where she had been but no warm something was there. He looked for his projection-it was gone too. Curly had a bad feeling in the pit of his stomach. Where was she? This had never happened before, and Cubby and Sniff were asking him, where was the big warm one?

They were looking to him for help because after all, he was big brother. Fatty was for once not complaining but Ling Lang and Dusty Rose wanted to know. Curly told his litter mates that when he awakened the big warm one was gone and that's all he knew. Curly was very wise and he understood they had to be quiet so he told them to be very still and make no sound at all. There was danger very close. Now, he knew nothing of danger but he felt it. Curly told the pups of the danger close by and told them to be still and make no sound he said the big warm one would be back she had told him they must just wait. The warm one returned just before dark and stayed with the pups for two days.

The she wolf eased herself away from the sleeping pups; it was time to go. She needed water and food, or food for her young would run low. Mother wolf slid out the opening and stopped, every sense alert, she tasted the wind and found no sign of danger. She looked far away, then close and found nothing to disturb her. Down the draw she trotted, moving with the ground-eating smooth stride her breed was known for. A mile or so southeast of the den she found a seep of water that was good, and not too far from the pups. A mile or so west she saw movement. A pair of coyotes was running a big jack rabbit. She saw opportunity. She ran west, dropped into the dry wash and turned upstream. The big jack had also scrambled into the wash, only going down stream. Looking over his shoulder to see if the coyotes were fooled, the jack came around the corner and saw the wolf too late to turn back. He ran straight into the wolf's waiting jaws. There was one shriek, then silence.

The two coyotes knew what had happened for they had smelled wolf. They stopped as if shot, then made tracks as fast as possible to get away from there, anywhere, as long as it was far. A wolf would sooner kill a coyote fast as or faster than a rabbit and they knew the law. Mother wolf smiled to herself; the rabbit was good - a juicy, tender young one that would get no older because he had failed the test and had been careless. In the wild, the foolish ones never become grandfathers. Mother wolf ran home in an irregular pattern, not wanting to leave a path to her door. On the way, she looked for other game signs for food was a never ending process; she would have to hunt every sun or so until the pups could go with her.

Sniff heard her mother's footsteps before the other pups, and she told Curly the big warm one is coming! Then mother was there and she lay down, gathering her young and feeding them. Curly found his projection and drank and drank as they all did. Fatty was his old self, getting his food and more if he could, and this time it was Sniff's turn to bite him in the ear. When they had eaten their entire fill, Cubby asked; "Curly why is it so dark"?

I don't know. I ask the warm - one she will know said Curly.

Mother yawned, smiled and said your eyes are not ready to see yet. In a few days your eyes will open just enough to see a little light then soon enough you will see as all wolves see. Your life will depend on your eyes and your ears, but mostly your nose; you will learn to read the wind: it will tell you were to find food, water and whether your enemies are close. If you are careless you will be killed and then you will be gone because that's the law.

All day she loafed around the den, watching and cleaning them, then feeding them and watching them fill out. Soon their eyes would open then she would have problems keeping them out of trouble. Curly's eyes opened first, going from all dark to a slit of frighteningly blinding light. He pushed his face in mother's fur and whimpered; the big warm one licked his face and told him the hurt would only last a short time then he would see. Now you will have to help me with the others; if I am not here when it happens to the rest you must comfort them, as I have you.

Curly spent the next few hours enjoying his sight as he learned to distinguish shapes. His mother was a large shape and his litter mates were small, and he was confused - things were still dark I will ask mother he thought. Mother why are things still dark? She looked wise, got up and gently picked him up and carried him to the door; he looked out for the first time. Outside all was white except a few patches of ground. Mother it is white out there.

That is snow - it is still winter. Snow is cold and you are too small to be out in it.

Curly still was confused: but you go out there.

Yes I do but look at my legs: they are long and strong. Yours are little and short you would get stuck.

Will my legs stay short?

No. Mother took him back and put him with the others, now rest and grow strong very soon I will go, I must find food. I may be gone a long time I may not find food as fast as I did the first time now come and eat again. Minutes later she was gone.

She went out to find the weather had changed. It was colder. The wind was blowing snow, moving it at a faster pace. She loped down to the seep and drank, and the water was slightly frozen. She got it open and drank her fill. It was not going to be this easy next time. She turned into the wind and sniffed the air, searching for something to kill or already killed. Nothing. She ran southeast to the river, turned upstream and into the timber where it was a little warmer, out of the wind. That was a good sign.

She moved around the logs and standing timber, keeping the wind in her face, sniffing and testing the wind. It was full dark now, movement, a mouse she swallowed it in one gulp, not much but something. She ran out into a clearing, more movement, a young coyote was attacking a porcupine. She crouched low, waiting, for she knew the breed: one or two quills in the wrong place could kill her pups and her too. The coyote was not making much progress, so he turned to go and trotted of a few paces. The porcupine, thinking he was safe unrolled himself and started off. The coyote struck quickly, hooking his claws in the under side of the porcupine and ripping out his guts. The porcupine wailed in pain and died.

The coyote was very hungry and failed the test: he was not careful because he never saw the wolf. She bit his neck viciously, killing him. Now what to do? She solved the problem and carefully ate the porcupine avoiding the quills gathered up the young coyote and started back to her den it was cold now and snow was falling the wind was blowing causing a blizzard she knew were to go she stopped by the seep the water was froze so she ate snow at the den she had to dig out the opening she pulled in the coyote and put it to one side. It was fairly warm and snug in the den, she went to her pups cleaned them, feed them and went to sleep. All the next day the snow fell and the wind blew on into the night she had been lucky there would have been no hunting in a blizzard they would had to make due.

Cubby's eyes opened, followed closely by Ling Lang's soon they all would see, and before the next day they did. The coyote was all but gone, and no brake in the weather the she wolf was getting nervous. She was not in trouble yet but soon would be. The pups were growing fast demanding more food, and no one to help. Her mate had been killed by a lucky arrow launched at the last minute just before he crossed the ridge. The unlucky happening had been three days before the New Year.

Some brave was wearing, a new fur head piece with out a care for the she wolf. The wolf went to the opening and dug. The snow was deep and it took along time to break out, when she did her world had changed. The snow had drifted over the over hang half covering the plum patch. It had stopped snowing but the wind still blew. She sniffed the wind, no game but no enemies either she went inside gathered her young and feed them. She finished eating the coyote and rested.

Curly knew soon she would go, he begun to dread his mothers going he knew he was in charge in her absence, and what could he do? Mother sat up she looked at them turned her head and looked wise. "Curly will be charge while I am gone he is first born and a male. You must listen to him. He is wise, he will sense danger. If he says make no sound then be still if you are discovered and I am not here then you will be killed just like your father that's the law." I am the only one who can find food kill it and bring it back to feed you, there is no one else. Your father would have but, an Indian killed him for his fur coat. There are others like that they kill us for our furs and meat but we do the same. I have been lucky I have found food fast and brought it to you.

There is much snow, it will take time. I will break through the snow; I can not run fast and will miss often. If I find a large something it will be good, then he will go through and I will catch him faster. You are safe in the den just as long as you stay here. Out side you will freeze and be no more. This is also the law we live or die by the law. You must be brave I may be gone long, or short. Know if I am alive I will come to you. Come I will feed you, then I will go, no one said any thing then Curly spoke" Let us cuddle together we will stay warmer, we should sleep the time will pass faster."

The she wolf sniffed the wind. She tested it from all sides nothing, she ran North West into the wind. The snow was hard moving in places it was soft in others hard, it was cold and full dark she did not mind her nose was guiding her. She ran the ridges. The snow had blown off making travel faster. She remembered a cedar draw thick and snug. It would be ten miles or so, when she got there. She slowed to a walk entered the woods stopped and sat under a large cedar.

She sniffed again then listened, at first she though she was wrong, such a small sound, only a brushing of some thing on a tree. Now she smelled, it was a very large mule deer, a buck. He was large, maybe to large. She could see him now, his antlers was like a tree. He had not seen her, yet she looked close he was not alone. Two does were there and a year young one. She made up her mind; the young one had to be her mark. They were bedded down, looking up the draw what luck, she studied them, and she needed to get closer.

The wind was coming from them to her that was good. She slid low making no sound. She got above and behind them. Just a little more she froze in position. She needed to break the young deer's neck the first try if she could. She had no idea if the old ones would turn on her or not. It was a chance she must take. She gathered herself and sprang. She felt the neck bone snap then leaped clear. The other deer came to their feet, snorted then bounded away. They were gone. The fawn was struggling to rise to stricken to get much done, she finished it.

She ate her fill until she was, gorged. When she got back to the den she would regurgitate, her way of taking meat home. She was cleaver for her breed. She removed the hind quarters from the deer, rested ate snow. She then ate some more. She then picked up the two quarters and started back. It had been a very good night.

Traveling was slow. It was better on the ridges. Light was coloring the east, when she got to the over hang, tired but satisfied. She dropped one quarter and took the other in. Then came out got the other, and took it in she had deer meat for three days. She feed the pups and went to sleep she was dog tired.

She awakened with the sun, three paw span over the horizon. Mother Wolf got up and called the pups." I have some thing for you, (she regurgitated some small piles of half digested deer meat.) This is your first meat this is what we eat all our lives" Curly ate a little meat, than it was Cubby's turn. He tried some, good very good. The two brothers looked at each other, a bond was forming. Hunting is what they would do. It was a way of life. It was life. The rest of that day and most of the next the pups wrestled. They rolled and pulled at each other, making growling sounds only stopping when it was time to eat, then at it again. Mother looked on and smiled she was pleased. This was how it should be; the pups were growing fast, almost to fast.

The light coming from out side was like a magnet drawing them to it. She got up and stood by the opening. She said "listen to me not one of you are to go past the opening until it is time then I will take you. Out there are things that fly called hawks, they want to eat you. They come out of the air you never see them. There are white small things that crawl fast they also run called weasels they want your blood. They bite your neck, then drink all your blood and kill you. Then there are badgers bigger and stronger almost a match for me. You are safe as long as they can't see you, smell you, or hear you. That's why I keep the den clean by eating the droppings, and besides the snow is deep. You would be lost; your legs are to short. Obey me and live to see world go out and you will die that is the law." Dusty Rose asked." Curly who made the law? I don't know. Why don't you ask Mother? No one thing made the law. It is a rule to live by that works for all.

Suns were getting longer, next morning the sun had more power, the wind was down and the air had lost its bite. The snow was settling, a peaceful calm had come over the land. It was the time of year the Indians called the awakening moon.

Chapter Two

Three weeks had passed, hunting had been slow but enough. The she wolf went out at first light, tested the wind made a full circle. She found nothing to disturb her. The snow had almost disappeared, except in the deep draws and large drifts. It was time, to get the pups. Mother trotted back to the den, went inside and spoke to her pups. "We will go now. Stay close to me, do not go in front of me, or fan out to far on either side of me. We are a pack of wolfs now. Curly will run on my right, Cubby will be on my left, Fatty will run on Curly's right and Ling Lank will run on Cubby's left Sniff and Dusty Rose will stay close to my hind quarters. When we go out do as I do." She turned and slid out of the opening. The pups fell in their appointed places running with that smooth gait all other beings envy and admire, it is effortlessly.

The long stringy muscles coiling and uncoiling, making the ground slide away. She stopped at the seep that was now a stream they all drank deep. "Now rest a little and look around you, do you smell any thing?" "Curly sniffed I do smell something, what is it? "Skunk" mother said. Is it good to eat Curly asked? Yes, you can eat it but we do not because of his unpleasant smell, and were a skunk has been it is safe to walk, so we leave him go but if you are hungry enough he can be killed quite easy, but remember in the spring he is many times sick. He has a poison that makes him run in circles bite at every thing even a bear. He can not drink water, and soon he is dead. Even then leave him be the poison can be still be there and if you eat him you may die. Are you tired? No came a course of little voices then let us run, get in your running spot."

She looked from left to right all were running in order. She lead them south east to the Moreau River let them splash in the water near the bank where small fish were swimming. Dusty Rose batted one out on the bank with a lucky swing, the sun fish flopped, the little wolf pounced on it and ate it. Now it was game, they all were fishing. Curly caught one Dusty Rose caught two more. Mother saw a swirl in deeper water she pounced and caught a large cat fish, and put it on the shore. She killed the fish opened it up so the pups could eat. They had never tasted any thing so good. She was lucky she caught two more big fish, than took them away from the river to some buck brush and cherry thickets. She bedded them down and gave them milk. It was warm in the sun they were tired and all slept.

She did not go back to the den that day or the next. The weather was not bad and they needed the exposure. She lead them up country, through the brakes and up on the flat lands, hunting as they traveled. She saw buffalo far off and some close, all big animals nothing she dared to kill. She stopped sat down and called the pups to her." They are meat. Two or three big wolfs would kill one but you are to little, you can not help me yet. But soon we will try on smaller game. Does any one smell food? No, get in your spots and we will run sniff the wind as we go." Cubby asked, "what is that smell Mother? "Food", she smiled.

Over the next rise she stopped them. "Look do not move, see everything. Two white shapes lie on the ground, look far, and look close. Do you see any thing? No now look up what do you see? Two large birds were gliding above the shapes, eagles. They can kill you. If you were alone they may still try, let us go." The shapes were skinned buffalo as she knew; most of the meat was gone. Indians killed them two days ago, now eat there is plenty still for us. She put them in their running spots and took them as fast to the north by east as they could go. The cedar draw was her goal and three hours later they were in the snug covers of the cedars. This is where she had killed the mule fawn.

She took them down the draw, past the shattered bones and hair of the fawn, to water all drank deep. She had run them hard. Mother wolf knew that she could travel about 20 miles an hour for long periods of time. She was always fleet of foot, and could out distance her litter mates in any given contest. She remembered with a nod to herself. First, she wanted to check their wind to see if they could keep up with her. The flats made her uneasy. To open and no place to get caught out away from shelter this was the time of quick snow storms. It was the fifth night away from the den. She found a spot in a low place were the branches were so dense she could barely get in. Much old leaves and grass littered the ground. She feed her young milk snuggled down with them and slept.

Curly was a large pup, long of leg with a silver gray coat, trimmed with dark guard hair that started from his ears down his neck, over his shoulders to a thin line down his broad back over his rump on down his up curved tail. His eyes were bright and intelligent, his muzzle long and broad. His teeth were long deep set and snow white. His under side was tan mixed with white he had dark lines down all four legs, with a white patch on his chest that went between his front legs. He was wise beyond his nine weeks sure footed and quick and looked so much like his father had looked, mother was glad. Her son was so much like her lost mate. She missed him, and if she ever saw the Indian with the fur head piece. She meant to kill him she would know that fur anywhere. Curley was tall almost as tall as the she wolf and weighed nearly sixty pounds about half as much as he would weigh when full grown. He could run at her side all day and not drop back. He was a son to make a mother proud, yet Curly was obedient, never trying to take over the pack, although he could. He never went past her, always staying back a half of a head behind her when they ran. She was the boss and he meant to see all knew that.

Cubby was burly big and long slightly bigger then Curly and weighed a bit more, but to him Curly was big brother and that was that. Cubby was dark in color. His face was almost black with dark gray marking separating his features. Cubby was over all charcoal gray, with black guard hair running about the same color pattern as Curly's. His under belly was lighter gray with modeled dark gray patches, on his front feet the tips of his toes were white, the only white on his body. Cubby had yellow eyes that gleamed out of his dark, face making him look evil, but in fact he was kind if a wolf can be kind, he loved his pack members and hated his enemies, killed and ate his food and when he growled it was terrible to hear. He did it mostly to amuse himself. But to a young weasel he caught snooping around the watering place it was the sound of doom. The weasel soiled him self getting a way Cubby laughed and laughed and when he told Curly later they both laughed, even mother smiled. Mother then smilingly said, "Maybe we should let Cubby lead the pack in the hunt. His terrible growl will remove the bad tasting residue from the game making them better tasting, all thought this was funny", except Fatty. Who, had just worked out a cactus thorn from his paw.

Fatty was not as tall as his two brothers, but he was husky, broad and just as fast as the others. He to could run all day and all night if mother said to. All Fatty heard when he was little was the law. The law this and the law that, now mothers word was the law. She had hit him with her paw. Several times for disobeying and that was enough. Fatty would climb a tree if she said to, Fatty was lighter colored then Curly, and he was light gray almost white his markings were the wolf markings. Down between his ears and down his muzzle a dark gray mark appeared it went around his eyes and stopped half way down his cheek, he had ears that stood up and were pointed at the top, his eyes were keen he could see far. He had a bad disposition when he showed his teeth and when he growled he was not pleasant to look at. Fatty ate to fast that gave him gas on the run he let it go and his sisters who ran behind him looked at each other wrinkling up their noses and said wind just passed again.

Ling Lang was a lopper, in other words his gate was a bounding stride much like the mule deer used, don't get me wrong, he could stretch out and fly over the ground maybe the fast one of the litter. He was tall and long his hair was smooth and silky almost white in color, his eyes were a pail yellow with a greenish high light. His muzzle long and well shaped. He had a habit of lifting his lips just enough that his fangs showed when running sending fear to the one in front friend or game.

Link Lang was edgy, coming to full alert at the smallest sound. Nothing was going to take him by surprise. He had the habit of licking his nose and lips. Ling Lang was mostly white with the blending of light brown hair giving a Buffy appearance. He had a peculiar dark tip to a other wise white tail, on either side of his rump were light gray strips that came together to form a gray line up his back only to spread out again up over his broad shoulders, his under side was a silver white with gray brown lines going down the outside of each long leg. He ran at Cubby's left side because that is where mother told him to run and no one argued with mother. His over all scent was dusty rain. If you recall, when you were young and the ground was dry and a little shower of rain came by, the very first drops that fell on the dry ground smelled like, "Dusty rain".

Sniff ran on the right side of mother's rear leg, just behind Fatty. Why? Because that's were mother wanted her to run she wanted no mistakes she wanted to know were they were, at all times. Sniff was smaller then her brothers, she weighed only forty two pounds at nine weeks about half the size she would be, but she was quick, nimble and strong. No one was going to leave her behind, and they didn't, she could run all day and all night with nothing to drink but the wind and nothing to eat but the distance. She was wolf gray in color, not as deep gray as Cubby, but darker then Curly.

Sniff had high erect ears, her eyes was set wide apart golden brown in color, her fangs was long and as sharp as needles, it is said that a full grown wolf can break the leg bone of a buffalo. A dark gray pattern started behind her ears, down her neck spread out over her shoulders, down her back it narrowed, only to get wider over her rump then come together again at her tail and stop. Her tail was up curled with a dark gray tip, her under side was a light gray mixed with tan, this color run between her front legs and up her chest part way then stopped. Her legs were gray brown in color, with white gray that started under her flanks and run down on the inside of her leg to the feet. She was alight weight whirl wind, over there, over here, now where, oops she had you by the butt you could not keep track of her. Sniff had a sent like wind in the far away.

You must stop and think, have you ever stood on a hill top on the South Dakota high prairie on a mild early spring day, no wind then a breeze comes from no where mixed with the smell of growing grass, first blooms a meadow lark singing way off. That's wind in the far away. If your answer is no then may be you should.

Dusty Rose was the last of the litter to be born. She was tiny at birth and a little weak but had gained strength fast. Now at nine weeks she weighed just a little more then her sister Sniff, just as fast on the run but a little shy. She would rather stand back and let the others kill and maul the game, but she could and had. She knew in order to eat. Game must die that was the law. A law was harsh but the law anyway.

Dusty Rose was shorter than and not as long as her brothers but average for a little she wolf. Her color over all, was a reddish brown with white inter mixed though out, her ears was erect tan trimmed with black a brown gray patch of color came down her fore head just below her eyes then changed to white and tan. This dark color went over her eyes down her face back to her neck. Down her muzzle, ran gray lines to her black nose, the rest of her face was tan and white. Dark gray lines went from between her ears ending by her eyes. The brown gray color went up to the top of her neck back and over her shoulders to come to a line down her back over her rump ending with a dark tip on her tail. The rest of her was red tan with lighter color running down her legs, under her flanks and belly up between her front legs a gray brown color appeared ending there.

On each side of her hips a small gray patch blended in to the red tan. Her eyes were yellow tan, for far seeing, and clear, her nose sharp and her ears had average hearing. Dusty Rose had one feature the other wolves had not gained yet. The hair on her neck stood tall and hung down on either side forming a main, similar to what a horse had. This gave her neck a thicker appearance and made her look more menacing. She on the other hand did not feel fierce. Her nature was gentle shading closely to being kind. She did not hate the prey or the game. She only killed them because it was necessary to eat and she did like to eat. Curly and Cubby killed the game indifferently almost mechanically. When the game was killed she always felt a little remorse. For, like I said she had a kind nature but she was a wolf and was guided by her wolf instinct. So she said nothing about her feelings to the others. They would have thought her weak. She did not want to feel weak in front of her siblings. Her scent was grass after a summer rain. You, the reader wherever you live have I'm sure smelled grass on your lawn or beside a road going through the country or out anywhere has smelled the pleasant odor of green things growing after a shower. This is how Dusty Rose smelled.

They had jumped a doe, mule deer an hour before dawn, coming out of the cedars. She was alone, and the pack knew why, she was lame her left fore leg was hurt not bad enough to stop her, but slowing enough to keep her out of the herd. Mother wolf slid low, calling the pack around, Curly, "Cubby and Sniff go to the right and drive the doe into that draw were all those rock are, run her hard this will injure her more. Fatty you Ling Lang and Dusty Rose go left she will run in to you about were the draw gets steep, you first three fan out to keep her going so she goes up the rocky draw and not to ether side, you second three come down the sloop fast, she will whirl around right into the fangs of the first three, flank her on two sides one of you get her throat tear it open and let the blood drain as I have taught you.

I will stay here and watch, do it right or you will go hungry I may not always be with you, I will be with you as long as I live but remember your father was killed for his fur it may happen to any of us, now go." Curly took his gang at a fast lope down the hill, mother sent Fatty and his two left over the hill to be at top of the draw when the deer got there. The mule deer was frantic. She could not run well. She should have stayed with Bounder the big buck this morning when he suggested it, but she was not her self she wanted to be alone for a few days to recover from her fall. "Bounder", maybe she could call bounder he might get here in time, over and up the draw she would dash then call Bounder. Then the other wolfs were there, she turned fast but her bad leg did not work well she felt fangs on her flanks then on her neck. Bounder, where was Bounder? It was getting dark and no Bounder. Mother wolf trotted down to the kill it was a clean kill no nonsense, all ate well, by mid morning they were finished.

Mother was pleased her pack had done well; they watered at the stream rested, ate more then started for the den. They did not really need it any more but it was there. The under belly of the she wolf was trim again she had not feed her young for some time. They were ten or eleven weeks old she was not sure, kind of lost tract of time, the pack came up the hill above the over hang all dropped down.

She moved back to peer over the crest. On the first flat above the Moreau River sat the cone shaped lodges of the Sioux eight or ten of them. A herd of horses forty or more grazed close by things that walked on two legs moved around the lodges carrying branches and logs, others were bending over something that was red and yellow and made a flickering light. There was round something's above the red and yellow flickering light that smelled good even at this distance. "Food from the fire pits." Mother said, "Stay away from them, they are men. One of them killed your father. They have a stick, the ends are tied together it throws a smaller stick that goes to fast to see, that smaller killed your father from a long way off. Get their scent and remember it. They are very clever they hide loops in paths that catch you around your neck and hold you, also around your leg." Why mother?" "To kill you, for your fur and meat, what are the big ones they are horses the man things set on them and go very fast far away. We will watch, and not get too close and we will not let them see us, they have dogs." "What are dogs?" "They are like us. They work for the man things. If we go close to the camp, they will give us away."

Chapter Three

Tall Elk sat on his deer skin, cross legged in front of the fire absently shaping an arrow shaft. Sweet Grass his wife was cooking the evening meal. His son, Moon Boy, who was six summers, sat across the fire from his father holding his throwing club, I missed two rabbits with the throwing club today father, both were close but they looked far away. Sweet Grass glanced at her husband and said nothing, Tall Elk worked a little more on the arrow put it down and looked at his son.

The Great Spirit has given you eyes that may be he was not quite done with yet. May be he wants you to finish them for him. Sun has carried his torch far to the west, and soon it will be dark. Go to sleep, and rest. When he returns with the light we will talk of it more. Tall Elk was sad how he could make his son understand some thing he knew nothing of, May Flower their two year old had perfect vision she could see well from the time she walked, he hoped Moon Boy would grow out of it and see.

Eagle Claw, tapped on the lodge cover and was bid enter, he sat down cross legged by the fire across from Tall Elk the guest remained silent, the host must speak first, as Tall Elk did. "Ho, my brother." Eagle Claw then removed his wolf skin head piece, spit in the fire an act that made Sweet Grass frown. Spitting was for out side not in her home was the brave stupid? Tall Elk cleared his wind pipe and spoke. "My wife hopes you will spit out side next time and not in the fire."

Eagle Claw was not nice. When he was hunting all the hunters wished he was in camp, and when he was in camp they all wished he was hunting. Eagle Claw said I think there is a pact of wolfs in our hunting grounds I saw their sign on the ridge. Tall Elk looked at his guest. "Leave them be do not disturb them, they may be our spirit guides. I see you are wearing that wolf skin head piece, why, it is not cold and you may make them angry if they are our guides all the game may go from here. The people have made me head chief of this band and I say do not hunt them. If you do I will send you away." Eagle Claw was angry he liked to kill and he did not much care what, he stood up to go looked at Sweet Grass and said "humph".

Sun up found Tall Elk and Moon Boy walking along the river each carried a throwing stick. "How far is that rock"? Asked the Father, "Throw your club the club spun, short. I see, you must throw and aim a little more then you do usually now try again, the club spun hitting the rock." Tall Elk smiled. "Now we will have rabbit and grouse in our stew pot" The chief and his son walked back to camp happy. Moon Boy had seen a jack rabbit sitting by some sage and his club spun. The boy had a hard time carrying the jack and his club back to camp.

The wolves stayed on the ridge until full dark watching the camp. They saw how the fire lighted up everything. How the fire made the food in the round things steam and smells so good. " Mother could we do that?" "No it is not our way, we can not make fire." Curly said, "mother that thing that walks on two legs has fur on his top part is it fathers?" "Yes the she wolf said I would know it any were." She crouched lower up came her lips, her longs fangs gleamed white in the night a low snarl slid out her mouth, her young was glad she was not looking at them. "We will watch and wait when that one goes off alone we will follow. When it is far enough away from the rest of them we will kill it. It will have something in its two things up by its top. It may have the stick tied at two ends that throws small sticks very fast, or it may have big stick like the one we saw at first light that killed the rabbit. It may have the sharp thing that looks like a long fang it will cut us, we must plan."

Chapter Four

Mother, called them to her; "When it is far enough away from the rest, Sniff will stay back and watch, if the others come fast she will tell us. The rest of us will come up on its back side Curly will grab the thing on the right side, Cubby will get the left it is very important that you do not let go or it will find one of its things and hurt us. Fatty you get the leg on the right side where it is large bite as deep as you can and hold it then it can not move around. Ling Lang you do the same on the left. Dusty Rose leap up on its back and get its long hair in your fangs and pull it over back wards. I will cut its throat so all its blood comes out. Now let us rest."

An hour before first light Eagle Claw come out of his lodge started to catch his horse, thought better of it and trotted up past the over hang. Over the ridge north west, going in a straight line, to the cedar draw where the mule deer were. Eagle Claw had his bow and quiver on his back. In his right hand he balanced his club. His knife was in its sheath at his side. Eagle Claw felt good. He fully intended to kill a wolf or two, or may be a mule deer he did not care, as long as he shed blood. Tall Elk could go jump in a dung pile if he did not like it and if the rest sent him away he would laugh in their faces. Eagle Claw smiled and if Sweet Grass said anything he would show her to.

Eagle Claw was looking far ahead, he should have looked behind he heard the dashing feet too late. He was going to turn around when

Curly got his right wrist at the same time. Cubby got his left Fatty slashed his right leg and hung on. Ling Lang tore his left leg to the bone and held him. Eagle Claws club was tore away from him. Dusty Rose did her job she jumped on his back and pulled his head back. His scream was awful, five wolfs had him pinned he was cut to rags and the big one stood over him her fangs dripping the pain oh the pain now he know now he remembered all the things he had killed just for the fun of it. His bow not even strung he had no hand to get his knife and now the big wolf he knew it was her mate he had killed to make the fur cap. She cut his throat and killed him.

"Go wash in the stream she barked a short bark." Sniff came running she barked again and they all came. She got the cap put it up side down on the braves chest and told them to all put dung in it they did she last it was full. Now we must go, and go fast, we have killed one of them, get in your running spots let us go and go they did. It was five hours later or about a hundred miles she let them rest. They were on water shed far south west. About dawn they killed a buffalo calf and ate it all, she found a snug cedar draw got under cover and rested.

Dove Tail, Eagle Claws wife tapped on the lodge cover of Tall Elk, and was bid enter. She was given the place of a guest. Dove Tail was offered food and drink. She ate and drank a little to be polite. Tall Elk looked at his guest and waited for her to speak. Dove Tail sat with down cast eyes and she looked up. "Eagle Claw has been gone from the lodge one sun, he is not back. I think he went to kill a wolf or a deer or anything that will spill blood. He was very angry." Tall Elk looked at his guest, "I asked him not to hunt the pack they may be our spirit guides. If we anger them all the game may leave." Dove Tail said. "Will you look for him?" "Yes we will give him two more suns to get over being angry, than we will go." Dove Tail got up to go, "Thank you my chief."

Two suns had gone by. Eagle Claw had not returned. On the morning of the third sun, Tall Elk asked five braves to go with him they mounted their horses and rode out of camp up past the over hang, over the ridge and to the North West. They rode five miles or so and saw the crows and mage pies. They kicked their mounts to a lope and soon found Eagle Claw, just as the pack had left him, except the meat eating birds had tore him up some. Tall Elk saw the fur cap still full on his chest with the wolf dung in it. Ho, Tall Elk said the wolf cap was one of theirs now they are avenged. No one liked Eagle Claw any way so no one felt too badly.

The chief asked two braves to go back to camp and get some thing to put his remains in. They got his club; knife, his bow and quiver than they sat down to wait for the others to return. It did not take long for the others to return. Doves Tail was with them. She would want to see where Eagle Claw was killed and see why. The cap with the wolf dung explained it all. We will take him back to camp and put him on a scaffold. Maybe our spirit guides will forget their anger and help us. We will say no more of Eagle Claw. He was bad anyway.

The pack, stayed long in their beds. It was a hard sun, just past. First they stalked and killed the bad man thing, which killed their father. Then had run a long way fast to get out of that place. Now they were in a new place. All had eaten well and were not hungry yet. Mother stood and sniffed the wind. Some thing was not as she liked it. More man things were moving a long line of them. She put them in their running places and took them north east at a long lope. Are we going back? "Yes, I like it there better we can watch and stay out of sight, here is all strange to us. We will run until the sun is half past mid point, all of you look for food as we go."

Over the next rise, all stopped and crouched low. In the draw below them a young buffalo cow was giving birth to her calf. Her first and may be her last. All was not well, the calf was coming wrong. The head was turned back and she could not move it. The cow got to her feet hunched over and strained, no good. She lay down and strained, nothing no movement. The cow's energy was all but gone. She gave a low sound like a wail almost a cry and panted to weak to move.

The she wolf told the pack to stay. She got up and went to the cow. She circled around sniffed the calf was dead. The cow to tired to care. She called: "Curly and Cubby come here. Each of you get a hold of 'a leg and pull I will pull it by the neck now pull, out slid the calf. We will go back to the hill and wait." Presently the cow very shaken, got to her feet. She smelled the calf. The wolf and cow looked at each other a long time. Understanding past between them the cow shook her head and moved off not looking back. The calf was still. When the cow had gone off a ways, mother said "now we will eat the calf and they did"

The day was almost gone when the pack finished their meal. She took them north by east at a long swinging lope that covered ground as by magic. Soon they were back at the cedar draw once again. The pack drank at the stream and could see the man thing was gone. Good they were not going to eat it anyway it was bad. They went to the low spot under cedars and bedded down. Early April was cool, but that was good. They had the fur coats Mother Nature had given them. At dawn they were looking at the Sioux camp all was as it was. No! There was some thing different a long thing was in the tree, she could smell it the dead man thing she and her pack had killed. Why, it was safe the pack would never eat it, in fact they would never go near it. They would sooner eat sick skunk with the poison that made skunk run in circles, only to die.

Chapter Five

Tall Elk entered his lodge, bringing an arm load of wood for the fire. Sweet Grass was helping May Flower put a new dress on her doll. She looked up at her husband and smiled. Tall Elk was a good man. The band had chosen well. He was a splendid choice for chief. He looked at his wife and little girl and was pleased. He only wished his son could see well. Maybe he would as he grew older. He spoke, "I think our spirit guides are back. I saw them on the ridge this morning, they were hiding but I saw them any way." "Is it good, my husband?" "Yes to have them near is good luck." "But they killed Eagle Claw she reminded him, he was bad I would have killed him some day myself or some one from another band would have, he was kill crazy he loved to kill.

Did you see how he looked at you the other night?" I almost followed him and killed him then I was afraid of what he might do to you and the little ones, now let us speak of him no more." Sweet Grass was quiet a long time, then she spoke, "I am afraid for Doves Tail, she is alone how will she live? Maybe she could live in our lodge." "Go and ask her to come, we will speak of it together." Sweet Grass was only gone a short time, when she retuned Doves Tale was with her. She was given the place of a guest; Tall Elk cleared his wind pipe and spoke. "After your time of mourning is past, we wish you would live in this lodge with us I have spoken." Doves Tail sat with down cast eyes for a polite time then she spoke. "My time of mourning will be short I did not love Eagle Claw, my father took four horses and two robes in exchange for me, I am glad he is dead. He told me that he would enjoy killing me, just to see my blood run, he was crazy I think.

The pack did us a favor, I would move to your lodge now but it would look bad. So I will wait one week then I will come." The two young women hugged each other. "It is good I will have help now with the children Sweet Grass said, "And maybe more", the girls looked at Tall Elk and giggled he was filling his pipe and made no comment.

In the new light of the new day Tall Elk asked ten braves to hunt with him, when all was ready they caught up their buffalo runners and rode out of Camp. "We will only kill Bull buffalo the cows are having their young and we must leave them alone. The wolf pack is with us again if we see them act like they are not there, they are our spirit guides, I think." The men rode with the wind at their back. They knew that buffalo grazed into the wind to keep fly off their faces, so in fact they were meeting each other. Eight miles or so east of the camp around the bend of the river a sizable heard of buffalo were grazing going north west. Tall Elk and the hunters sat on a hill watching the big animals move, all fanned out. "Each of you goes in among them and kill a yearling bull, two if you can then help any one who needs help. We will kill as many buffalo as we have fingers and toes on one brave."

Getting ready, they strung their bows and readied the lances, moved out and fanned out into the herd, all did. An hour later twenty one buffalo were down, bled out and the skinning had begun. The women got there cut up the meat, placing it on pole drags and started back to camp. All was done before sun was half way to sun down. In camp fires were lighted and hump ribs were roasting. Drying racks set up sagging under the weight of the kill. Every one had a job. Young children kept dogs from taking meat off the racks or tending fires under cooking pots all would eat well this night.

The she wolf, and the others, saw the horse's brought in to the camp. Something important was taking place. Dry skins were placed on the horses backs, raw hide strings were put in the horse's mouths and tied in place. When all was ready the man things hopped on the horse's backs and sat there holding the stick that was tied at two ends. The little sticks were in a bag on their backs. Some had a long stick with long sharp fang at one end, made of a rock or some thing, it was awesome to see.

One of them raised his right thing and pointed, kicked his horse and all moved out, to the south east along the river at a fast lope. The pack stayed on the ridge keeping them in sight, and kept them self out of sight they thought, Tall Elk looked at Bears Tail and smiled that she wolf thinks we do not see her good. The pack saw the buffalo and knew why the man things had come to kill buffalo. That was very good; when they were gone the pack would eat all as it should be. They lay down on the hill top and rested. They had not long to wait, soon the man things and horses were there. Tall Elk pointed and the killing began. She wolf saw the long stick go in a buffalo it fell kicking and before it lay still two more lay dead from the same long stick.

"That was some thing to remember." Curly said "why do they kill so many, mother?" There are a lot of them to eat, and they do not take only what they want, so it takes a lot to feed them. Very wasteful Sniff said," "Yes mother nodded very," but all right it meant more to eat fore them with less work.

Soon the killing was done, and the meat was on way to their camp. Come said the she wolf. Now it is our turn. Tall Elk turned and looked back, the pack was coming to the kill, now he knew just how clever the she wolf was. She would bring the game close he would kill it and all would eat. He was right she was good luck to have around, that bad one had almost spoiled it all, but no matter he would not trouble them again. They found the leavings more then enough, in fact, much more. Tall Elk had asked the cleaners to cut small piles of liver, lung, and kidney in plain sight for the wolf pack to find, as you may say a piece offering.

The she wolf was amazed, not only was the leaving much, it was of high quality piles, of the best meat was left for them, liver a much desired treat was mixed in the piles. May be the man things were not all bad. It could be that the man things had good ones among them just as other beings had. She knew of a wolf pack like that a wolf so bad no one could be near him and the rest good. They ate all they could, and went back to the hill top to rest, there would be food for a week or more.

Sun stood half way to sun down on the seventh day when Dove Tail came to Tall Elks lodge. She brought all of her belongings which were not much. Her sleeping robe an extra deer skin dress her cooking stones, the long flint bone handled knife, the bow and quiver with a few arrows, Eagle Claw was lazy and seldom had more then a few arrows at any time. Doves Tail was about to knock on the lodge cover when Sweet Grass opened the flap and said. "This is your home now you do not need to ask to enter. Dove Tail smiled and said, "thank you". Sweet Grass showed her where to put her things.

Out side was a fine early April day warm and mild. Some boys with Moon Boy had gone of to hunt rabbit with the club. Tall Elk and some braves were looking for beaver sign along the Moreau River others were doing this and that enjoying the day. The she wolf got to her feet and sniffed the air. She froze. Some thing was not as it should be no air, still, nothing moving. Ling Lang knew it to. What was it? The sun was gone as if it had fallen from the sky. An air current cold as ice swirled then more. Mother said "we must go to the den fast". Big drops of rain begin to fall and the wind was blowing now. "Run" mother said, "In your spots let us go fast".

Tall Elk and the braves turned back to camp the boys started for camp. Snow was falling like a curtain over the land. Mother Nature had caught them all, with their pants down. Tall Elk and the braves had three miles to get to camp. It took two hours to get there and when he entered his lodge Sweet Grass was in tears. "Moon Boy took his club to hunt rabbit and never came back." "Was he alone" Tall Elk asked?" "No, two boys went with him. "Are they back"? Yes, he must have got lost. Who were the boys? She told him". He got some robes and went out in the storm.

Tall Elk asked the boys. "When was the last time you saw him they did not know. How far did you go? Don't know. When you came back, was the snow hitting you in the face, left side?" He had some idea were to start looking. She wolf heard a sound far off, and dim a man thing child was crying. "We will help", she said "spread out if you find it, howl we will come and help". Curly and Cubby found the boy not far from the man thing camp they gave the howl the others were soon there. Curly get on his right side Cubby on his left. The she wolf put an arm over the back of each side of the two wolves. She pushed from the back side. They were close now. Tall Elk was there. He saw at a glance the pack had saved his son. He picked up the boy turned to thank the pack they were gone. He carried the boy to his lodge and put him by the fire, he then went to tell the braves.

The pack had saved my son. When he got to the lodge Moon Boy was sitting up. "Father, two wolves found me. I was not afraid; they brought me to the lodge. Why father? They killed Eagle Claw and saved me." Tall Elk turned to the women, tears streaming down his face. "Fix us some food, I will try to explain. Moon Boy, my son you are very young. Your heart is as pour as the snow falling out side, you have no bad or evil thoughts in your mind. You love all things.

Eagle Claw, was bad, in his heart was only evil, he hated all things even himself, he even hated his wife Doves Tail, who is now part of our lodge, she is kind and good that is why I asked to be my second wife and to share our lives. The she wolf saw him kill her mate, for no reason, only to see him die. She could see in his heart it was all cloudy and evil, because he was evil. Do you understand my son? Yes father I think I do."

"All your life, the wolf will be spirit guide for you, for wolf saved your life, and you must protect his. Later you must learn the names of the two wolves that saved you, then their eyes will become your eyes and you will see far as they do, and when you hunt Curly will be on your right and Cubby will be on your left and men will follow you.

The three of you together will be great for then you will see both sides of the ridge at once. You will have six eyes to see with, all others will only have two." "But father I do not know their names."" You will. I see it in my mind when the storm is over we will take food to their den, stay there and wait they will come." "I do not know how to get to the den." "I will show you it is not far." Outside the storm raged, snow fell and the wind picked up the snow in huge arm full and flung it at the lodge till it shock. The smoke hole had to be moved often. Someone had to go to the wood pile and get wood it was cold.

May Flower asked, "Mother if it would end soon her doll was cold, she snuggled close and pulled up the robe. Dolly and I was going to pick flowers today mother, but snow covered them up, I was giving them to you and Doves Tail, now I cant, are you sorry mother?" "No I will love them when you do pick them." It was dark and the wind still blew, the fire was banked and all slept Tall Elk slid out of his sleeping robe got wood and stirred the fire. He placed bark, twigs and other bigger branches on, and then breathed gently on the coals. Soon little tongues of flam were licking at the wood he then put more and larger wood soon a fire was blazing .Tall Elk adjusted the smoke flap, and discovered the wind was down, the blizzard was over, and better yet when he looked out the east was clear. Sun would carry his torch and warm the land, soon little rivers of melted snow water would join the waters of the Moreau River, rushing down stream to the Missouri River on down to the Mississippi River onto the Sea.

But Tall Elk was not concerned about were the waters gone after leaving the land. The braves needed to check the horse heard. Pull fire wood out of the bottoms and make sure the arrow points were set firm in case big cat came calling. Tall Elk put on his buffalo coat, his knee length boots and went out. Sun was coming over the eastern hills, all ready it was warmer, large drifts of snow were every where. Tall Elk called to the camp crier. "Ask the men to come to my lodge in one hour we should have a short counsel."

At the appointed hour all the braves of the band were assembled at Tall Elks lodge, except those few who Mother Nature, had called by necessity out on the slope out of sight of the camp. Tall Elk cleared his wind pipe and spoke, "my brothers, the wolf pack has given us back my son who would have been lost to us in the big snow. They are our spirit guides. They bring game close for us to kill and now they guided my son to the lodge in the storm a wolf on each side and one pushing from the back the rest showing the way. No one is to disturb them in any way. I Tall Elk will meet anyone in combat for not hearing my words I have spoken". "And I Brings Plenty Horse, stand with our chief I saw the wolves bring in Moon Boy. I was looking also." All the braves said "Ho we hear you.

We should go and look at the horse heard and may be pull in wood for the fires some horse could help, look for sign of big cat he may be hungry he likes horse, may be he should eat rabbit, tell him that if you see him. Looking Back Horse, Iron People and Taken Alive saw to the horse heard, the others got axes and raw hide ropes and went to get wood. Some of the young women went to help it was warmer now. By the time sun had gone almost to sun down the wood pile was replenished, horse was fine and no one had seen anything of big cat, snow was settling some water had started to run.

When sun brings his torch back at first light, Tall Elk said, "you and I will take some food to the den I will leave you, then you Moon Boy will speak to your spirit guide in your own way, you will make friends and they will trust you I think, now we will eat and rest at first light we will see. When light came the father and son were near the den they put the food down and Tall Elk got up to go, the camp is there sit a while and wait we will see."

The man thing and the small one we helped are coming, they are carrying some thing, in what they call hands it smells good I think it is food. The two are sitting the big one got up, the small one is still sitting, what does it mean mother?" "We are not in danger, just wait we will see; small one can not see well I think, mother said," "we may have to help him again. Curly said Cubby let us go and set near him so eagle doesn't hurt him." Moon Boy was about to go back when two wolves come and sat near. Moon Boys heart beat fast they looked in each others eyes a long time, and some thing like understanding past between them. Moon Boy was not afraid. He got up and got some of the meat. The wolves looked curious was the small one going to eat the meat? No he was offering the meat to them, he came close to them holding out the meat, it was their turn to be afraid he was not big and offered no threat. So they waited. "Eat it mother said coming out of the den, he wants you to have it" Curly sniffed, and ate it. Good. Cubby smelled his and ate his. Good, now the rest of the pack stood and ate apiece or two.

Moon Boy put his hand on Curly head and patted it, good it felt good. The boy did the same to Cubby good. The rest of the pack was shy. Two wolves at a time were enough. Moon Boy started back to camp, it had been quite a day. On the way to camp Moon Boy discovered a wolf on his right he looked in his eyes an inner voice said. "I am Curly. I will be your friend. I will help you." On his left walked a wolf. "I am Cubby. "I am also your friend, we my brother Curly and I will help you and so will the pack, I think." Moon Boy put an arm on the neck of each of his new friends and proudly walked to camp, the pack followed. At the lodge Tall Elk waited arms folded on his chest a smile on his face." You have done well my son, who is your friends. Moon Boy patted Curly on the head. "This is Curly my spirit guide. This is Cubby he is also my spirit guide. They told me in a voice only I can understand no one else will know, they will help me only when I need help, the rest of the time, they will be wolves, it is good." Tall Elk knelt down and looked deep in to Curly face their eyes locked. "Thank you my brother, for saving the life of my son," Curly smiled and nodded his understanding. Tall Elk also thanked Cubby, he nodded his understanding, are my friends hungry?

The two wolves sat down and licked their lips. Tall Elk smiled and gave them meat. They just looked at it but did not eat. "What is wrong father?" The man was puzzled then he saw the wolves look from the meat to Moon Boy back to him Ho he said, and got food for the boy. When the boy ate, so did the wolves. The rest of the pack was close now sitting in a group, but back a ways. Tall Elk took them food, after all, they had helped bring Moon Boy to the lodge and they were part of the pack. He hoped they would feel welcome.

Now most of the band sat or stood observing the wolves. Brings plenty horses came and stood by Tall Elk it is good my chief, we lost one bad one and gained seven good members to our band it is good. Yes very good Tall Elk nodded. Iron People asked. "My chief, are there not other wolves in our hunting grounds? How will we know them from our brothers? Iron People have asked a good question, I will ask my son to ask Curly his spirit guide, he will know." Moon Boy, looked long in Curly eyes much understanding passed between them, Curly asked, the she wolf the question, she smiled and replied we know the bands property and they are safe from us.

We may eat a dead colt but only if it is dead. We will tell others of our kind not to hunt anything of the bands and if a wolf is bothering horse it will not be one of us." Moon Boy said, "The pack told me, they would not hurt anything of the bands, and if a wolf is bothering horse it would not be one of them. Curly said they would tell others of the wolf kind to not hunt horse, and the only horse they would eat would be dead." Moon Boy said the pack were proud to be brothers of the band.

The she wolf stood up and made sign to go, and they were gone. Tall Elk and men of the band talked for a while more and agreed that the horse heard was safe from their pack but would watch for stray wolves Moon Boy spoke and said; "he was sure the pack would watch also. The snow was melting fast and soon it would be gone. We will wait two suns then go look for beaver along the Moreau River beaver's fur is best now and his tail will be good in the stew pots, all said "good we will go". An hour before dawn Curly and Cubby came rushing to Tall Elks lodge each gave a howl. Tall Elk come out of his robes like they were on fire. He saw the two wolves and he knew some thing was wrong. Curly looked past the chief inside the lodge. Moon Boy came out and the boy and wolf exchanged looks. Father, "some strange braves are coming, they have sticks tied at two ends more little sticks that go fast and the long stick with the fang on one end. Their faces are red and yellow with bird feathers in the hair. There are as many as the pack and three more. Go my son call the braves to the lodge."

Tall Elk got dressed got his bow, filled his quiver, got his lance and went out side. "Moon Boy you must come to. You can speak to our spirit guides the braves were all ready." "Cubby had gone to watch", the boy said the rest of the pack are there already. Moon Boy ask; "Curly where are they?" The boy and wolf looked at each other.

In cedar draw ten miles west by north. Twenty seven braves and one boy rode out of camp, about five miles from camp. Cubby waited. They are just getting up the boy said." Tall Elk told the boy, have the pack spook the horses so all is in turmoil then we will hit them. The pack exploded the horses. Braves were running every where, when the Sioux hit them.

It was over hardly before it started, all nine braves were down. "Go catch the horses they came to take ours, now we have all their horses were caught and tied." Tall Elk and the others went to look at the downed braves; two were killed by ax blows to the head, five with arrows, and one by Tall Elks lance. The last man was not dead only out cold. Tie this one. Get your arrows you shot, all so out of the dead men. Gather their bows and arrows, their lances, their knives and axes they came to take ours now we will take theirs. They will need them no more. Tall Elk sat down exhausted. He told his son. "Thank our spirit guides without them we and our families would be dead and our lodges burned." Moon Boy and Curly looked long in to each others eyes. Curly told the pack who nodded and were gone. The dead braves were laid out in a line. They would be put on scaffolds later.

The captured brave was awake now. He was put on a horse and went with the Sioux back to camp. Back in camp the older braves and the women had set up a defense line, just in case the Sioux braves were not the victors. When the men came over hill, leading the extra mounts, and all were back safe and accounted for, a cheer went up that could be heard two miles away or more. The bound brave was helped of the horse and put on the ground. All the gear was put away the horses rubbed down and turned out to grass except the few kept tied just in case.

A morning meal was cooked and eaten. Tall Elk got to his feet. "Hear me my brothers we would be dead and our camp burned if my sons spirit guides Curly and Cubby had not come and told us of the approaching enemy. We owe our lives to them, and the lives of our loved ones, give thanks to them and to the Great Spirit I have spoken". All said "Ho". They had put the captured Crow brave in the spare lodge of the late eagle claw. They had lighted a fire and retied him.

Tall Elk and two braves went to see him. Untie his hands we will talk, the crow brave was young only a boy, but old enough to come and kill. Tall Elk asked, with the hand sign, "how are you called? Bird Wing, why did you come"? To kill you and take your horses and your young women if they were pretty enough. "Why should we let you live"? My father would give plenty horse for me. "Why so you can come back and steal them again? Sweet Grass brought some food and drink, now eat then you will be retied. Outside Tall Elk asked what should we do with him? Looking Back Horse said, "let him help put them on trees, then send him back to his country on foot and if he comes again he is first to die, he owe one life to us. Get the Crow horses and let us look at them, when the horses were brought in.

Tall Elk called Moon Boy my son, you have been on your first war party at six summers. Now I give you a horse I give you this bay pony with white for feet. Take good care of him, there was brown and write pinto stud that Iron People liked take him then. The rest was chosen until all had new owners. Ten of you, get some lashing, get the crow he must walk and you my son mount your horse, we will put the dead in trees and send the crow back to his country, now let us go."

Moon Boy went to the wood pile got up on a log and swung up on the bays back he side stepped a little but moved out well. Moon Boy rode beside his father, the crow brave ran in front, Tall Elk had striped the young crow leaving only his foot gear and breach clothe. Bird Wing knew he was lucky he should be dead with the others; the raid had been badly planed from the start. What was supposed to be a weak camp of Sioux, under the leadership of a mild chief, with few braves turned out to be a wild bunch of fearless men fighting like a pack of wolves?

Speaking of wolves where had the wolves come from? That was not part of the plan, now the war parity all were dead, but for him. How would he explain that if he ever got back? And if that was not bad enough, they lost all the horses and weapons, and he a chief's son was running almost naked. He wished he had been killed, and then he would not have to explain. Now they were at the fight place and he saw the dead, he was sick. They made him lift and push logs in place forming a platform, now they took the hair. All of them put the braves on the platform covered them and tied the covering in place. It was awful!

The boy sat on his bay horse with the white for legs that he Bird Wing had raised from a colt. He burned with rage, he would come back, he would show them, and he would get a new war party they would pay. Now Tall Elk the chief pointed a finger at him and said, with the sign talk. "Now small boy go home and never come back or I will kill you, I should kill you now, but you are too young to die, so I give to you your life back, now you owe me a life." The chief pointed west and said go, the boy made a barking sound and a pack of wolves were there all around him. The worst of it, the boy jumped off his horse got face to face with the big brutes and spoke to them, and the wolves knew what he said and spoke back.

The crows legs turned to water he was too frightened to run they were all demons. He wished he had never heard of this raid. A large black and gray wolf came up to him opened his mouth and growled such a terrible growl that he began to run, up over the hill and over the next. He ran blindly with out reason, he could not stop. Bird Wing looked back they were all around him fangs showing white and the boy on his horse lopping along behind laughing. He discovered water was dripping off between his legs and it was not sweat. Gone was the thought of revenge he was done with this country, he would never come back no mater how many bay horses he lost. He looked back Great Spirit they were still there; spots were spinning before his eyes. He had stopped dripping from between his legs now he dripped from all over now that stopped to. All went black he fell exhausted. To tired to care he lay still water he would like water, war parties, no never again. If the war trail was like this he would pass, medicine man yes or a helper of women having young any thing, with this he fell to blissful sleep.

Moon Boy and the pack chased the dashing crow brave for twenty miles or so, or until he passed out. He called to Curly all turned around and they loped back to the cedar draw. The bay horse was accustomed to the pack now, so made no fuss at their nearness. Moon Boy was tired it had been a very long sun, starting before day light the bay did not like the blood smell and wanted to run, so they ran. The bay horse was fleet of foot it took a short time to run to camp, his father met him at the lodge took the bay and turn it loose to graze.

Chapter Six

Mother wolf asked Curly and Cubby to go look for food. She and the pack were in cedar draw resting. When you find something to eat call us. We will come, call us with two short wolf calls. Curly and Cubby found an old buffalo cow this time it was the cow that had not survived. She had bleed to death in calving her calf stood by, head hanging and forlorn it would not last long with out milk. Curly and Cubby gave the two wolf calls. That got the notice of a buffalo cow not far a way, she saw the wolves and came running bellowing and making a fuss. The calf hungry nuzzled the cow and drank deep. The cow always had two calves this year she had one, now she had two, the two wolves had saved the calves life.

The cow took her new baby, and went to find her other calf. The two wolves smiled, all was well. The pack had come and all ate on the old cow, who in dieing had feed the pack. This known as the food chain, grass grows, cow eats grass, wolves eat cow and what is left goes to ground that feeds grass and so on. It was dark; the pack had feed well, and was resting after their meal, Curly said, "Cubby, you should practice growling more then we would not have to work so hard. You would run of all the bad man things that come to bother our band and our friend Moon Boy. Did you see how the bad man thing ran so fast that he soiled him self?" "Yes said Cubby, I think he is running yet, looking and looking over his shoulder, he may be has run into a tree and killed himself by now, saving us the trouble."

The she wolf was cleaning herself, she looked wise, "I don't think this trouble is over yet other bands of strange man things are moving around just he's not she's they come to kill and steal horse from our friends. I think two hours before light, we should run in pairs going fast ten miles or so around our band, Curly and Cubby, you run one way, Fatty, Sniff and Ling Lang go fast the other way Dusty Rose and I will run the little in side circle around the camp. No one should be able to get past us. Your nose, your ears, and your eyes use them all if any of you find any thing go to Moon Boy." so they get ready then give one long wolf call, we will come together and plan.

When Tall Elk hunts he gives us much food, now we will help the camp by not letting the bad ones get in. About two hours before light the wolves were on patrol they ran as the she wolf had laid it out. They ran fast and with out sound every sense alert. They moved like spirits over the land not a thing was missed, or a sound or a smell nothing. When they were finished, the pack was above the camp by the den. "Now let us rest, but one of us stays awake till dawn, I will" Dusty Rose said and she did. A little past dawn the camp came awake, fires were kindled and food cooked a new sun had began.

Curly and Cubby went to report they found Tall Elk making water behind his lodge he greeted them. "Ho my friends I will get Moon Boy the two wolves nodded." Soon Moon Boy was there, tell your father the pack was on patrol before dawn and found no bad man things close to camp, or any place near, the two of them looked long in to each others eyes the she wolf said." There are man things moving around all he kind, no she kind. We will look and watch we are your brothers." Moon Boy told Tall Elk all, the chief looked long at their spirit guides and said. "Thank you Curly and Cubby we will rest better. Are you hungry? Curly licked his lips and sat down, as did Cubby call the rest they did, after all had eaten.

Tall Elk called a short counsel, my brothers our spirit guides has been on patrol and found no enemies close or far from camp, but the she wolf feels other war parties may be coming, my brothers no band has ever had this kind of help before, I ask you, should we ask other Sioux to join us for a season? Think on it, and spend some time making arrows and longer bows. The bows from the crows are not like ours they are thicker, longer I have tried one of them, they send an arrow farther faster then ours do. Maybe we could try to make some better bows and let our women shoot to we may need there help if the enemies are too many, I ask your wisdom."

Taken Alive got to his feet." My chief, when word gets around, that we killed some crow braves, and lost no one, I think others will want to join us, but I will make more arrows and may be we could show the older boys to shoot." "Iron People said my brothers son would come and bring his lodge and may be his good friend Spotted Owl too, I think it good to make more war weapons if we don't need them good. Looking Back Horse said, "my chief, it was a good day when our spirit guides, joined us every one is safer now I ask Moon Boy to thank them, I would be good to have more lodges but it will take more food, can our hunting grounds feed more lodges, if so, how many more."

One Skunk asked; "I am going to the ash trees to get bow sticks some people could come and help bring them back, my bows are strong and send arrows far I would help some one make a new bow. My wife is nervous, now she is not so nervous, I sleep better I would like to know I would make a bow for the wolves but could they hit any thing, this is what I would like to know." All smiled One Skunk had a way with words.

Two days had gone by when Skunk, You Can Not See and his lodge and family came and asked Tall Elk where he should stand the lodge? "Iron People my father's brothers are here and we could come and hunt and fight with you, so we are here. I have some friends, who are coming also; Yellow Footed Dog and Spotted Owl will be here soon with their lodges." "Good" Tall Elk called Moon Boy call our spirit guides, he did, and the pack was there. "Tell Curly two more lodges are coming they are our friends also they will live and hunt with us.

Skunk, You Can Not See was showed the pack, they are our spirit guides, and they told us about the crows coming to kill us, so we killed them first." "Ho" the Skunk said. "That night the wolves ran a larger circle, going west twenty miles then splitting four, running south and three going north by east then running east and then south to join the other four. A military genius could not have done better.

The south four turned east, then turned north and came together. When all was together again, Sniff said she smelled wood smoke. She thought on south run, they rested a little and then went to look about five miles or so they all smelled smoke. In an ash draw were some crow braves painted for war, eight of them in all." Curly and Cubby raced to camp, At Tall Elk lodge Curly howled two times, Tall Elk and Moon Boy came out, as many as the pack an one more are coming, they have the red and black color on their face and bird feathers in the hair. "Son call the braves tell them to get ready fast." Tall Elk came out of his lodge Moon Boy get your bay, you must go and talk with our spirit guides, he handed his son a lance ask Curly were are they. Moon Boy said twenty miles south west, let us go. Thirty braves road out of camp.

Curly was in front; Cubby half way and the rest of the pack at the crow camp. Ten miles they found Cubby and Sniff. She had come to tell them the crow was a sleep. Good it will be easy. They road fast until they were all most at the camp. They circled the camp and moved in. The crow were jerked out of their blankets, tied hand and foot and put in a pile to wait for light. The Sioux ate the food that the crow had and rested.

The horses grazed soon it would be time to teach the crow braves not to bother a Sioux camp, that was not bothering them. A lesson not many would remember, how could they. Most would be in happy hunting ground, not caring about horses or scalps. In the east a rose color had spread first light had come over the land, not in a hurry the Sioux waited for full day. Bring in the horses.

Tall Elk liked a big blue roan stud. I will take this one, a crow brave Winsted but said nothing Tall Elk walked over to him and told him in sign talk. "If you had stayed in your own country and not bothered ours you would still have him." Tall Elk picked up braves bow and quiver and handed them to his son, when you are ready you can use them, he will need them no more. Gather up all their war things let us go.

Put them on horses facing back so they can see they are leaving their country for last time, tie feet under horses belly lets go. And they did. Tall Elk and the Sioux road in camp all were glad no one was hurt. The crow was set by the wood pile to wait. Tall Elk and his head men went to talk with the crow. "Who is chief here?" "I am Turning Rock leader of this war party, why are you here?" "To kill Sioux braves and take horse, we have done you no harm Tall Elk said," "Now you, Turning Rock will be killed. Where are you and your main band from? We are from Yellow Tails band on the east side of the tall mountains, Yellow Tail is father of Bird Wing the brave you sent home in disgrace.

We sent him home, alive. We told him you are too young to die go use your life wisely. If you come again you will die," Turning Rock said, " Birds Wing has given up the war trail, your spirit guides took away his manhood, he is afraid to go make water. Yellow Tail sent him away. To us he is already dead. The only way he can undo that is to kill you Tall Elk and he will and the wolf pack." "Tall Elk said that is a tall dream, and will not be. You other seven, did you want to come and why. We thought your band of Sioux were weak we thought it would be easy, and now Tall Elk said?" "You are not weak. Five of you will not go back, two will, you will tell Yellow Tail, that if any more of your band comes to kill not any of them will return, and then I will go to kill him I am tired of getting up when I should be sleeping, to out in the dark and catch and kill dumb people who should have stayed in their own camp in the first place. Tall Elk got to his feet, and walked over to the captives, two were young he chose them you will live to go back to tell Yellow Tail my words. Moon Boy call our spirit guides, he did.

They were standing by the boy as if by magic, all the captives' eyes were wide, so was their mouths, wide open. Turning Rock, your thoughts were low on our spirit guides. You did not believe Bird Wing, now you must face them. Tall Elk cut Turning Rock free and took him in the open space. Moon Boy tells Curly what we would have him and pack do.

The boy looked long into his eyes, this brave came to kill us all now you and the pack kill him, and maybe no more will come. The pack knew, mother called the pack close. "Cubby, when we circle him, growl as only you can, make short jumps at him, Curly you and Ling Lang cut his legs from the back the rest of us cut him all over cut and jump clear don't kill him to soon." The brave was big, he had no weapon but he was a man and they were just animals, he smiled he would kill two or three just for the fun of it. They circled him fast, he turned with them, he grabbed, missed almost fell, better be careful that sound from a quite spin to a horrible growl, his blood froze he almost fell he wanted to run, no place to run. Now he knew what Bird Wing felt oh no he had wet himself. Cubby growled again.

Turning Rock turned he put out his hands, his legs were cut from butt to feet. He screamed, slash his arms his sides his back cut he fell blood all over. They had cut the tendons in his legs, no more war trails, no more blue roan stud. He got a hold of a wolf leg and tried to hang on the she wolf broke the arm. He screamed long the pain, the pain, then she cut his neck his blood was almost gone anyway. They had not seen Eagle Claw die. They only saw what was left, now all had seen how and they were shocked the captives had seen. All wide eyed, and terrified.

Tall Elk could turn them all free he knew not any of them would ever come back. Tall Elk untied the two come here and look, have you seen enough? Or would you like to see more. No we have seen, take of your close, keep your foot wear, they did. Do not stop, do not rest, and don't try to eat. Run till you find Yellow Tail tell what you saw, tell what I said in three suns some of us and our spirit guide will come looking for you. If we find you, the wolves will kill you. Do you understand? Yes, now go and go fast, they did. The two young men sprinted away like fine arrows from a strong bow and were soon gone.

Tall Elk walked over to the other five. "Who is next one of you who likes to come and kill people in their sleep old, young, little or big? Who, who is next to feel fangs in their sides, backs, and legs, they sat terrified, stunned unable to speak, three had already messed them selves, and you laughed at Bird Wing look at your self, are you better?" Tall Elk took the hair, untie them. "Take him down by the river and pile rocks on him he told the five and wash yourself you smell bad. Moon Boy get your bay ask our spirit guides to go with you, some of you go along see they don't run. A few braves went also.

The five enemies awkwardly carried the dead body of their chief; in fact, they did not want to touch it, all bloody, limp, and lifeless. It already had a bad smell he had fouled himself. The five were talking among them selves, in their own tongue. One Skunk made the sign for silence, all were quite. Iron People rode and had found a sandy bar of ground. He pointed and made the sign for digging. By now the five were as bloody as the body. All dug in soft sand until it was deep enough. When it was they rolled him in pushed it full of sand and carried rocks to cover it, they turned to go. One Skunk made the sign for more rocks, they started to complain. Moon Boy asked Cubby to growl his terrible growl and Ten Hands put more rocks on in a shorter time then twenty could have, in a long time. Let us say, the grave was adequate.

Moon Boy brought the captives back to the camp. Tall Elk signed that they were to set by the wood pile. Tall Elk and some head braves, gathered to talk to the captives. Tall Elk used sign talk, as they could not understand the others talk. You come to kill and steal, you failed. We killed your chief; we sent two of your young men back to tell Yellow Tail, and to tell him my words. Stand now and tell me how you are called. A tall young brave said "I am Runs Fast, I am Black Dog said another, I am Bulls Tail, said the third, I am called, Snake Tail," the last said, "I am, Looks Far. Tall Elk, asked should we let them be one of us? Or kill them?" "Tell them", said One Skunk. "If we take them as one of us and they try to run off or try to steal horse our spirit guides will kill them. They will be left as they fall. If they choose to become one of us they must work and do all things as we do. If one of them says no, I will run my lance into him right now. Ask them Tall Elk, if they want to live or die"! Tall Elk stood and asked the five in sign talk "we have spoke of this. We ask you, do you want to live or die? If you want to become one of us you must fight our enemies even if they are crow. You must learn our tongue and our ways. We will be your people. If any of you say no, you will be killed with the lance now! We wait for your words and your words must be your law! I have spoken".

The captives spoke among them selves, Runs Fast said, "I will live and be one of you. Looks Far said as I will, I Bulls Tail would live, and I Black Dog said no, I would die before I would be a Sioux. One Skunk killed him with his lance, Snake Tail, looked long at Black Dog who lay on the ground. I like the sun at first light, I like to eat, and set a good horse I would live and be a Sioux, "Ho" all said. Moon Boy called the pack, he showed them the new braves, smell them they are our friends now, they are part of us now. Tall Elk said. "Take this one and put it with the other, and then we will eat. I will place you in lodges so you can learn our tongue." The wolves knew the camp dogs now and tolerated them.

The dogs was not so sure, but were wise enough not to bother them. After the dead crow was disposed of, all ate. Tall Elk said, "When sun brings his torch to light our way I would like fifteen of you my brothers to go hunt bull buffalo with me." Iron People take some braves and look for beaver along the river his fur is good now and so is his tail. "Some of you stay close to camp and help One Skunk make bows, Moon Boy ask our spirit guides to watch, Yellow Tail will come I think, I just don't know when, or how many the boy and Curly, shared thoughts. The pack knew the importance of their mission. They had gained new braves, some not tried yet.

After dark had come, the pack loped west by a little north spread out looking for sign, missing nothing. At place of the buffalo cow they stopped and ate some, it was a little past prime and they were used to better, but they ate anyway. They stayed for an hour or so sniffing the air up above the cow the air was bad below. They ran west and then swung north, then west by south. Covering much land and found nothing. When the pack came to thunder butte they climbed it, they were seven hundred feet above plains below. The moon was shinning, and you could see a long way, they would rest a while. Mother yawned and said. "I will sleep, some of you watch."

It had been a long sun, so they did. Just before moon down, that is before the moon falls on the western edge of the world the pack got up and looked to the west. Long they looked and saw nothing. The she wolf said. "We go now, the crow may come from a different place and we are here in this place and not see them." So they ran very fast, east to the camp getting there at first light. Tall Elk was again making water behind his lodge when Curly got there and made him understand that he needed Moon Boy, so he could talk. Moon Boy was there. Curly told him all the pack had done, and had not found any enemies, coming from the west. "Are you hungry" asked Tall Elk?" Curly sat and licked his lips, call the others so he did, after they ate Moon Boy told him of the good buffalo hunt, and how much meat they had harvested. Curly nodded. "Good, some of us will rest others will watch, and when it dark the pack will patrol again. The camp had grown in the last few days. Spotted Owl and Yellow Footed Dog had stood their lodges with the others. It was said more were coming, but Sweet Grass was uneasy. She felt something was going to happen. She was not sure what, the band had more braves, the spirit guides was watching.

One Skunk had made some better bows, and arrows. Point maker and his helpers had crafted some fine points to fit on the new shafts still she was on edge. Why did the enemies have to come? Why not stay in their country. Had not enough of them died already? It was now the last days of April, Sweet Grass and May Flower walked on the rise above the camp. The little girl had a hand full of flowers she had picked, the flowers are for you and Doves Tail mother, "do you love them?" "Yes they are lovely." "Why do you look far away, mother? Are you looking for more flowers?" "No I think maybe the enemies are coming soon. They want to kill your father and all of us maybe." "Why? Mother, he is very good and they are very bad. Will our spirit guides help?" "Yes I think they will, I just wish we had more of them, come we must go back." Back at the lodge, Sweet Grass said, "My husband I would like to talk with our spirit guides, if Moon Boy would speak for me."

Tall Elk motioned to his son, who called his short bark and the pack was there. Sweet Grass got to her knees and looked long in to Curly eyes. "Son tell our spirit guides I feel the enemies are coming, they want to kill us. I think all of us. I am afraid I do not want to be a crow slave wife or my family killed or you killed either. I would ask that you watch well and not go too far in your patrol. They may come a different way." Curly looked at the she wolf, the she wolf looked wise and said. "Tell her we will know when they come; an eagle that I saved a long time is looking now the eagle will pay back the favor. Curly told all to Moon Boy and soon Sweet Grass knew and said. "Tell the eagle we will give her much food for helping us." She wolf said. "Good. I will tell her." Sun was past high point Tall Elk got food for the pack, when they ate their food; he looked long in their eyes. "Thank you my brothers, for your help." She wolf said "your enemies are now our enemies, together we will send some of them back in disgrace and others will not go back but rest in trees a very long time."

Chapter Seven

A dot came from the south west as it got closer, all could see it was eagle. Eagle circled floating on wide wings she sat down on stump and she wolf walked over to her. They talked for some time. Curly and Cubby went to. Curly and Cubby came and spoke to Moon Boy, eagle said riders are coming, ten and ten and five and one." Tall Elk said "call the braves all came." Eagle said," A large brave, with many of my relative's feathers in his hair, is in the front". He rides a black horse with white legs up to his knees, also one back leg, with white just above his hoof. The horse face has a white star between his eyes, he is nervous he throws his head from side to side. He has much power. All others are well horsed to. It will take two suns to get to this place I think. I will watch from my place in the sky. Tall Elk asked, "Is Eagle hungry?" Yes she would like meat, it was done. The chief called a counsel. My brothers he began, we now have a new helper thanks to the she wolf, and we have Eagle. I have said this before, but no band has ever had help like this before." "The enemies are coming eagle saw ten and ten and five and one all well horsed, they will be here in one sun, they come from the west. We must plan, Iron People you and Taken Alive are good planers give us your wisdom the two talked.

Iron People said, "We should meet them two miles from our camp. The good bow men can hide in a half circle, when in range all send arrows at the same time. The spirit guides can come from the back make a big sound. When the horses are rearing and plunging some bucking, our horse men can come down the hill in a line with ax club and lance. The rest of the bow people can come from two sides, shooting arrows fast. Try not to hit our braves. Some boys could come who have learned to shoot, some women to if they want to. The two stepped back and said "this is our wisdom, all said Ho". The chief said, "That is good plan. Are there others who would speck?" One Skunk spook, "I have some poison from snake, I could put a drop of it on arrow point let it dry it will make them very sick, they will not feel like fighting for a long time. I think, may be they will only want to sleep in trees like turkeys.

Looking Back Horse asked to speak. "May be two lines of horse men could come down the hill fast to finish of braves only wounded by the first." "Good thinking said Tall Elk, but we are not many, five braves in the last group may be enough spoke Looking Back Horse. Fill your quivers so that is done. Choose your best arrows, and use the best bows, the crow bows should be, they shot far all have strung bows even if you are a lance or ax brave. The best bow men, get in a group, so we know how many sixteen were in this band, how many are best with ax club and lance, ten were in this band, including the chief. We need six bow men. On each side of the fight how many are left? Eight more got in line some older braves. We will need a few boys three boys got in line". Tall Elk spoke, "my brothers, some of us may be killed. If you see two of them after one of us help him who needs help. Woman could help here all others who can shot defend the camp and the young. Get ready, tie your best horse at your lodge and know your places."

Tall Elk called his son. "Let us speak with our spirit guides, the pack was there. Tell Curly and the others, when the first arrows fly, spook their horses from two sides. Cubby can do it well, when all are plunging and confused the mounted braves will hit them from the front, side bow men will shoot stay back so no stray arrow finds you. If you see, one of ours in trouble slash the crow from all sides. Jump clear, ask eagle to watch from her spot in the sky. Keep watch when dark comes, but stay close to camp. Ask eagle to make noise in the fight, this will confused the enemies if they think she is with us. Meat was given to eagle and the pack, all was planed now they would wait and see.

The pack watched, but nothing was different, at dawn food was cooked and eaten. Fires were put out so it would be hard to burn the camp. The pack come and sat around the lodge, eagle flu of to the west. Two hours later she came back sat on the stump. She wolf went to her and eagle said, "They are coming, and should be at the camp, when sun is past midpoint."

Tall Elk and the braves, the spirit guides and eagle went west to wait. A long draw pointed at the camp. It was wide and shallow with sage and buck brush up near the rim here sixteen bow men hid all with plenty of arrows that One Skunk had put a drop of snake poison on. Just out of sight were Tall Elk and fifteen braves with ax club and lance. On each side of the draw were eleven more bow men, six on one side and five on the other. The pack were hiding in brush, the floor of the draw was grassed and smooth a good place to move quiet, around the bend rode a splendid group of horse men. They stopped and slid of their horses each one putting on war paint and other charms. A signal came from a tall brave with many feathers, all mounted and moved up the draw past midpoint, eagle circled making loud sounds. The first flight of arrows hit them all looking up, watching eagle the second on heels of the first put twelve braves down. Curly and Cubby with Fatty and Sniff, dove at the horses under sides the she wolf and the others came from the other side the horses went in the air plunging screaming and bucking. There were riders going off on all sides.

Tall Elk hit them then. Nine more crows were down arrows from the side cut two more. The crow leader and Tall Elk came at each other. Crash! The two horses hit. Tall Elk was on the ground the crow leaped at him with ax held high as the crow swung the club Tall Elk got him by his leg and tripped him while putting his knife in the crow killing him. The last two crow were tided and on the ground. It was over but not without cost. Six Sioux braves were killed, giving their lives to protect the others. Four crow were alive, tie them and get the horses all of them, Tall Elk said, "get the war gear to, he was still on the ground, a long cut on his arm, an arrow in his upper leg. Get the arrows you shot." The dead Sioux they put over their horses, the chief was helped on the big black others of Tall Elks band would have to be patched up. When they got to camp, the dead were laid out by Tall Elks lodge.

The woman began to wash and mend the cuts. The medicine man was burning sweet grass and other healing herbs and shaking rattles, driving off evil spirits. Tall Elk was the worse hurt. The arrow in his leg was stuck and had to be pushed on through then broke off then pulled out, he had lost a lot of blood. His cut on his arm was bad, the ax had cut him from shoulder to elbow but he would mend. Tall Elk called his son. "Call our spirit guides, he did the pack were slow in getting there.

Ling Lang was hurt he had an arrow low down in his left hind leg. Sweet Grass Dove Tail and Moon Boy went to him, the boy told him to lie still, so they could get the flying stick out. Ling Lang said, "That is what killed father, will I die?" "No. Your hurt is not bad, you will be good in few suns, all were given meat stay by my lodge so we can watch and see no evil spirit bother you." The scaffolds were ready. Tall Elk came out of his lodge helped by Sweet Grass and one brave, his face painted black in mourning for the loss of the braves. Bird Foot just fourteen shot arrows at the enemies. Wounding one, we will all miss him. Snake Tail our new brother, fought his old brothers, to save us, he was brave.

Fat legs forty two summers, rushed two crow one hit him with ax, we will miss him. Two Tall was with me as a boy, I and all of us will miss him. Big Tree was killed by a lance from a dying enemy. Hair Falling took an arrow in charging down the hill he was very brave. Now let us take them, so they can rest. They rapped them in robes then put them on the scaffolds, Tall Elk said, "If we say their names more, they will be angry." On the way back to camp, Sweet Grass said, "war! "I hate war many are hurt some die; all feel sad, enemies and us to why?" Tall Elk said nothing, she had said it all.

When all were at the chiefs lodge, Tall Elk seated on a robe, he said bring the horses, and they did. I will take the black with white legs half way up and star on his fore head. The rest were fine horses, pintos, bays, roans, white and cream color the braves picked until all were chosen. Tall Elk asked for the crow leader's bow and quiver and ax, the one that almost killed him. The bow was big long and thick it was different from the rest. It had strips of horn glued on it, which gave it much power; he could almost not pull it. One Skunk asked to look at it. He was the bow maker, he looked long, and he tested the pull. "Ho", he said horn strips make it very power full, I will try, we will see. Moon Boy held Ling Lang head in his lap wiping it with a cool deer skin. His head is warm father, may be he has the fever. Give him water to drink and may be some powdered willow bark. (Authors note.) Willow chewed works like aspirin, it may not help but it will not hurt him either. Sun has carried his torch far to the west, it will be dark soon.

We have had a long and painful sun. Give food and water to the captives retie them. One or two of you make sure they don't get free, when sun brings his torch again to the land we will make them put them in trees. Then we will see. Go rest and thank the Great Spirit for our victory this sun and our spirit guides also eagle. Tall Elk got up slowly; he hurt in many places, as did many of the braves. He came out of the lodge on his own power. His horse was waiting for him. Tall Elk called his son, "Moon Boy get your bay and come bring the wolves it was done, Ling Lang, you stay in camp, unless you feel like running." He stayed. The four crows walked; Curly on the right, Cubby on the left, the other for forming a neat half circle.

The crow wanted to run but knew it useless. Cubby slipped in close beside the brave on his right. His fangs gleaming, a low growl slid out between his exposed teeth. The brave belly turned to a block of ice, with no place to go. Why did he come on this war party? Bird Wing told them Tall Elk Sioux are killers and have demons helping them, go and you will die, twenty two had died. Now they were at the killing ground, bodies all over in every position. Blood all over and fly, they took the hair; there laid Fast Bull his brother's son, mounted on his blue roan stud he had raised from a colt, now some Sioux had him. He was sick, he knew them all. They made them put the bodies on a crude platform in a pile, then cover them with grass then logs. No way to treat good braves who fought well, and didn't want to go in the first place.

The trick of having eagle circle over head, screaming to get their notice; The arrows, not one or two arrows, but many arrows all hitting at the same time. Then the demons hit the horses exploding them into motion an unseating rider that is when Tall Elk came down the hill smashing in to them. With ax club and lance, not ready so many died at one time. Buffalo Tongue looked for a knife, a broken arrow anything to fight with. He could find nothing, they had been careful not to leave anything, and they took it all.

When the dirty job was done the wolves under the boy mounted on Bird Wings bay with white for feet. He took them back to camp, made them wash in a stream that was good they needed water anyway. The dead smell was making them all sick. When the word got back that Tall Elk was a Great War leader no chief would get any braves to follow him to raid, Sioux, under Tall Elk and the wolves. Who ever heard that wolves fighting along side of men? This is what Buffalo Tongue thought, as he and the others cleaned up after the fight. In camp they were made to sit by the wood pile, Tall Elk, and the braves came and looked at them.

The chief and the boy sat on horses taken from the crow that was good; they must think the horses were good anyway. Tall Elk said in sign talk. How are you called, I am Buffalo Tongue another said. I am called Horse Dung all smiled how did you earn a name like that? When I was young I threw horse dung at every one. I am called Badger Claw and I am called Big Bull. Tall Elk asked why you are here. Some of us did not want to, but our leader was angry. He wanted revenge for killing so many of us, and said we should go on the war trail with him, so some did. And now, how do you feel? I should have gone elk hunting in the mountains. Did you Buffalo Tongue kill any? I shot four arrows. We know one was in Bird Foot I am sorry. Would you be a Sioux like three of your brothers are? If you would take me yes. Badger Claw jumped up, women I would die first." So he did. Horse Dung, how do you choose? I will be a Sioux. Big Bull said, "I will join you Tall Elk you are very fair others would have killed us. Take that thing by your feet and take it to the pile in the tree put it there, when you have come we will eat. We are only Sioux here now, I have spoken. All who were there shouted Ho.

It is good some got horses they put the body over a horse the rest mounted and they took him to the pile it was his choice, no one felt bad. The she wolf came and sat by Ling Lang, he smiled sat up. I feel better mother, I am ready to run again the little stick that goes to fast to see did not kill me. You were lucky; we must be quicker next time.

Let us go run circle to the south and west by north and see. Curly told Moon Boy we go to make circle, if we see nothing we will hunt like wolves for a few suns. If you need us we will know.

The she wolf put them in their running spots now let us go. Like moon shadows they had completely disappeared just vanished. Curly ran on she wolf right, swift as a gliding arrow, soundless, and with out effort. Taking long ground eating strides, never missing a foot hold, every fiber every sense alert. Cubby ran on her left, eager to get the first glimpse of anything, game or enemies his eyes cut in to the dusk like flint knife made for sight. Fatty ran to the right most in his vision. He would see a mouse jump at fifty feet in full dark or hear a grass hopper change hold of grass blades at twenty feet.

They were keen well oil killing wolves, but you could not call them mean if they liked you they were gentle and kind. Ling Lang bonded like a mule deer, with no effort every long stride sure and quick. He saw every thing, heard every thing missed nothing. His eyes were keen, boring though dark like lightning bolts going though fog. Sniff ran low to the ground fast and sure she snarled as she run just for the fun of it. She was there and you never forgot it.

Dusty Rose ran at Ling Lang of left side, she was the left tail guard. If the others missed any thing she picked it up. The she wolf ran in front. Everything they were and more, around twenty miles a long boney ridge was there, so they sat on it and looked. The flat below was in darkness, clouds covered the moon a rift appeared and a shaft of moon light revealed buffalo bedded down, some standing on the plain below. Curly said. "Let us kill one of the smaller of them." Kill one that is hurt they are easy to kill mother said. We could look so they did.

A young bull got to his feet, a fore leg was broken, he had stepped in a badger hole when running other wise he was as strong as a bull, of course he was a bull. Mother said let us circle him, see how well he moves. Cut his tendons just above his back legs, and then he will fall. Fatty saw his chance and cut the bulls left hind leg. The bull bellowed whirled and fell, tried to rise only to fall again. Sniff Ling Lang and Dusty Rose opened his flank so the bulls in sides spilled out, he soon bleed to death. The wolves feed a long time on the hot nourishing meat, soon other meat eaters like coyote skunk badger even eagle would come and dine, very little ever was wasted.

It was early May and grass was growing as was all plant life. The air was mild and sweet with blooms of spring. All the wolves were bigger now and the males were seventy to seventy five pounds. The females had grown to around sixty pounds all sleek and well feed. Ling Lang was better now; he ran well only a slight limp that would pass. She wolf was ready, let us run up over the range to the south west, turning west at a fast lope by early dawn. They were west of Thunder Butte and had seen nothing of the enemies. They turned north and ran until two hours past dawn, swinging east getting back to camp when sun was two paws past mid point.

They went to Tall Elk lodge and sat down; Moon Boy came out and made much over them. Tall Elk sat on a robe by the lodge and listened. Curly looked long in to Moon Boy's eyes much understanding past between them. Curly told them of their run and had found no enemies in their country or new sign. Eagle was circling to the west and North West and had not seen anything maybe the enemies had enough of this band of Sioux. Tall Elk said, "thank you my brothers, I know we have you to thank for us still living and eagle to." Iron People nodded to the pack, and sat down my chief, how are your wounds? My arrow wound is bad, it pains the cut is healing we were lucky, our spirit guides told us how many, and when eagle told us where we could not fail. One Skunk walked up caring a bow.

My chief I have been working on this, look at it. Tall Elk took the bow, good it will work I think I would look at the crow bow. Sweet Grass brought it to One Skunk he tried the pull then the pull of his hmmm he said I think maybe I will warp it with wet raw hide. One Skunk said, "Maybe Curly could help, that is what I am thinking." Dove Tail said, "If the enemies are gone from our country do we need more bows?" "We need better bows" Tall Elk said. Even if to shot deer, if others have them we need them.

The mares had mostly foaled a good crop, the new horses taken from the war with the crow were studs a few gildings no mares, the studs were quarrelling, to see who would father the new crop of foals.

Iron People told the chief, some of the lesser studs we should tie to lodge poles and have the better studs father the colts. It is wise thinking, do it have some one help. Tall Elk asked his son, "Do you see well?" No father hmmm I see, at dawn ask our spirit guides to go with you. Take your bay with white for legs and ride the ridge over plain, ask the wolves to help you see more, take the bow and quiver I gave you and your throwing club. You may not need the bow, but get the feel of it. Have your mother send food be back before sun falls of the western world.

At dawn Moon Boy and the spirit guides with eagle soaring over head loped west by north; Curly on the right, Cubby on the left of the ridge, telling him what they saw. He saw two sides at the same time. Something no one had ever done be for. Moon Boy was glad he asked Fatty and Sniff to run in front now. He saw all with four pair of eyes to see with.

Sun was past mid point when eagle dove and caught a rabbit a young one. Moon Boy ate meat strips and all told the boy everything. It was good. Fatty up in the lead with Sniff told Moon Boy stop, old grandfather real snake is in your path. He is as long as I am and does not want to be disturbed. He will spook the bay you may got thrown, go around, do you see him? Moon Boy looked, yes and I hear him to, he is very old, Curly said. "You must learn to see with your ears. Old snake will tell you if you are to close, if you hear him sing, go around he only wants to be left alone."

Moon Boy turned south down a brushy draw. Curly and Cubby said, "Stop! Over that ledge is two mule deer a doe with her last year fawn. Can you hit with the stick tied at two ends? I can try, Moon Boy said. He slid off the bay got two arrows. Fit one on the string snuck up and peered over the ledge. The two deer stood by a cedar tree. Moon Boy pulled the bow and let fly. It was not a good shot but the young deer turned wrong, the arrow took it in the neck behind the ear, breaking his neck. Moon Boy was elated, his first kill. He put the other arrow back and scampered to the downed deer. Took his knife and bled the young deer. He removed the insides, which his spirit guides ate. Moon Boy got to the bays back, and said. "Curly and Cubby lift up the deer's hind legs the push he got a hold and pulled up came the deer. The horse did not like the blood smell but after some time he settled down. Let us go to camp. The bay wanted to run he still was not sure he liked what was on his back, but he trusted the boy. Tall Elk come out of the lodge saw the deer, and said Ho.

Tall Elk waved to all, my son has brought back his first kill a fine deer, come and eat in honor of Moon Boy the women skinned the deer Sweet Grass said. Deer skin I needed some the two young women grinned like they just discovered a grin. Moon Boy was served the largest portion all others ate some and said it was the best ever had. Later in the lodge Tall Elk asked his son "what did you learn"? Moon Boy said four wolves were in front I saw with four pair of eyes, Curly on my right Cubby on my left Fatty and Sniff in front we found grand father real snake, in my path Fatty and Sniff told me to see with my ears, I heard him sing then I saw him.

Good said the chief and the deer? Curly and Cubby said stop, over that ledge are two deer so I got the bow looked over the edge pulled and shot. One turned and the arrow took him behind the ear killed him, it was a lucky shot. How did you at six summers get him on your horse? Curly and Cubby each got a hind leg I got a hold of the legs and pulled. They pushed, up he come. Tall Elk said, my son I am very proud of you and your spirit guides they showed you more in one sun, then I could have in seven suns. We must hold a feast in their honor soon, Tall Elk held out the arrow this is the arrow that made your first kill. Put it some place safe, it will be your medicine arrow. Bring your quiver let us look to see how many arrows you have, ten we must make some.

Tall Elk said. "Come, they found Stone Barker, this young brave needs arrow points do you have some? Stone barker took out a leather bag and showed Moon Boy some white and blue flint points. "Ho good points." One Skunk was there, some one would help make the arrows if you want me to help. Yes the boy said. "I would." Good I will then. Tall Elk said when sun brings his torch back we will go kill some of bull buffalos. People we need liver lung and kidney for your spirit guides honor feast you my son will come we will see.

At dawn Tall Elk and Moon Boy got their horses and bows. We go to hunt buffalo; some one could help us hunt. Ten or so got their horses and gear, they were ready. The wind was from the north, so they rode south across the Moreau River. Two hours later the buffalo were there, a large heard, grazing in to the wind. Kill young bulls or dry cows we should have ten and ten and five or so. We will have an honor feast for our spirit guides and some rump roasts for us maybe some hump ribs to. "Ho" all said.

All spread out the buffalo paid them no notice. Twang a bow string sang and a dry cow fell. Moon Boy pulled the crow bow and hit a calf in the hind leg. "Ho" Tall Elk said his mother will spank you. He pulled the arrow free and gave it back to his son. Pull more hard and let it snap. This time the arrow took a young bull just behind his ribs to the feathers. The bull bellowed, lumbered off, went to his knees rolled over on his side, not dead but down. Stay on your horse, let the buffalo move off. This is not the time to be on two feet, you need four feet.

Twenty eight were down. New robes hump ribs and rump roasts. Moon Boys bull was still alive, but far gone. Tall Elk came and finished of the bull. This one will be one of the buffalo for your spirit guides feast. The skinning was started. When the cleaning party got there, soon all the meat was loaded on pole drags. Started back to camp, when they got there all came and got what was needed for their cooking fires. Moon Boy called his spirit guides they were there, Moon Boy told the pack. , that this feast was in their honor. For all the times the pack had saved the bands lives. A feast was put out for them, liver, lung, kidney and other meats all feasted.

The moon was shinning dimly, the she wolf snarled. She leaped to her feet. Ling Lang was up with her then the others. Down a ways big cat was slinking behind some sage and tall grass, intent on staking the horse heard. The pack was all around big cat, big cat was startled she snarled. "How you dare disturb me. I am going to kill a horse that one with white for legs will do." "No, that one is the horse of our friend Moon Boy. He is small and can not see well, he needs the horse." "Why are the man things your friends? Did not one of them kill your mate?" "Yes, and we killed him his heart was evil as yours is, I am killing that horse."

Cubby growled his terrible sound, big cats eyes opened wide she had heard other sounds but not like that. Go away big cat eat rabbit, they are more your style. Do not bother horse and maybe you will live. Big cat snarled then screeched, her back up I will eat horse and you to maybe. Fatty, Ling Lang, Sniff slashed her back side then jumped clear she turned in furry on them. The other four cut her on her unprotected side. Big cat screamed on them and got cut more. Blood ran from twenty cuts.

Two arrows hit her, then two more she was furious. A lance came out of the night cutting her though her heart, rabbit may be rabbit would have been better, to late no more time dark. Tall Elk looked down on big cat. Curly told Moon Boy she was going to kill the bay. Your bay! Moon Boy said, "I know father is there enough to skin"? "Yes, they say big cat is good to eat we will see." They carried her a short way to camp put wood on fires and skinned her. Tall Elk held up the skin. It was cut so many places it resembled a sieve.

We will remove the claws and make a necklace of them, to hang around my son neck. My son call your spirit guides I would look at them, they came. Ask if any of them are hurt, fighting a lion is no small thing, a few cuts and scratches, no more they were lucky. Moon Boy asked father? Could my bay stay by the lodge until sun brings his torch at dawn? Yes, I will go with you to get him can Curly and Cubby come to? Yes and the others to if you want, maybe the big cat had a brother Tall Elk smiled to himself may be. The bay was brought in and tied to a lodge pole, as an after thought the big black with white for legs all so came in, the wolf pack were some place close so all felt better.

Three more lodges of Sioux were seen coming from a way of, Tall Elk knew them from the big council last summer, all good braves. They were there when sun was four hours old. Ho my chief all said. We would join you Tall Elk and your band, it is said it is safe to be near you. Our enemies fear you. Your spirit guides, and also eagle. You are welcome Barking Bear, you Circle Eagle, and you Stands Tall. We are making better bows now One Skunk is our bow maker he would help, if you ask, I think. Stand your lodges near, then we could have a smoke and talk you could meet our spirit guides, they have saved us, many times also eagle. Barking Bear I see you have some girl child, good we have young braves who were crow. Now only Sioux live here, maybe you may be a grand father, some time. You are welcome. Circle Eagle you have many honors in your war bonnet that is good and some girl child to, you are welcome in our band.

Stands Tall, you are welcome, we can hunt and learn from each other of many things, I will show you the crow bows you could make some bows ,One Skunk will help, I think. Now my son will show all of you our spirit guides, Moon Boy called the pack, they were there. This is Curly, Cubby, Fatty, Link Lang, Sniff and Dusty Rose, also the She Wolf. They have found the enemies coming three times, and three times we killed them first. Except the last time when we lost six braves in battle. Two nights past they found and killed big cat, trying to kill horse, no band has ever had such help. Now they will help you, our new lodge people to be safe. All said, "Ho."

Chapter Eight

It was now the first part of May. The pack was most all shed off Curly still had patches of raged fur, but the rest looked sleek and trim Curly soon would. All the wolves had long hair on their necks now forming mains making them look bigger more fearsome, but in fact they felt no different. The she wolf got to her feet. We are getting lazy the sun was standing at mid point on a mild sun. We will run west to see what is bothering me. I feel more bad man things are going to bother our friends. Go tell Moon Boy, Curly Cubby and Sniff told him.

Tall Elk, the chief called a council our spirit guides feel more enemies are coming they go to look, may be we should get ready. Pass out the better bows and arrows. Maybe One Skunk could put the drop of snake poison on arrow tips, what dose that do? Asked Circle Eagle? Skunk said when we wound them a little they get very sick and don't want to fight no more, oh Ho we see. Tie your better horse near, be ready. The she wolf said let us run, so they did. On the trail the pack were alert gliding swift moving shadows, see all, know all, miss nothing, smell everything. They ran west spread out like a flying wedge. Near dusk they had went by Thunder Butte now swing a little south, on a hill top. Mother said, "Stop all lay down." "I hear something" Sniff said. I smell horse and man thing coming just one.

The brave slid of his horse made water stood a little, horse was very tired head drooping, the braves bow and quiver was on his horse, he sat down on a rock to let the horse rest. Should we kill him? No mother said, get on all sides of him, we will take him back to Tall Elk the brave was dozing when he looked up, seven wolves were looking in his face. Terrified the braves first thought was his bow no good, it was on the horse, he jumped up, Cubby pushed him down and growled his terrible growl the brave's mouth was open, but no sound came out. Done, no more anything, he sat like a baby.

They pushed him to his feet got him going east at a fast trot if he slowed down one of them nipped him. Sun was bringing his torch over the eastern hills when they had him in front of Tall Elks lodge. Curly barked a short bark and Tall Elk was there Ho he said. Moon Boy said to his father the spirit guides found him to the west, just him, no other so they brought him to you, good tell them thank you, and then get food for them. Yes father.

The chief called a council, when all were there he said, "Look what our spirit guides have brought us". All said "Ho". Tall Elk asked the brave "what are you called"? And why are you here?" "I am called Horse Dancer I come to scout a Sioux band under Tall Elk, Why? To learn their strength, I am Tall Elk, maybe you want to kill us in our sleep like the others did. They are dead, but for the few who are now Sioux. You have heard of our spirit guides? Yes, but we did not believe it. Now do you believe? Yes now if an old woman said go jump off a cliff I would do it.

Then an eagle came and sat on a stump the she wolf and Moon Boy talked to her long, Moon Boy told his father eagle said she saw, this one is the front runner to a large group of braves may be thirty or more, they are coming slow, they wait for this one, I think. Tall Elk took the brave's knife. Where is your bow and quiver? They are with my horse. With that two wolves brought the horse in to camp, Sniff held the lead rope in her mouth; Ling Lang kept the horse going. Horse Dancer was watching eagle, yes eagle is part of us we know what you do, before you do, maybe. Horse Dancers eyes and mouth was open, no it could not be, a dream, animals could not do things like this. How do you wish to die? Crow dog, maybe you could run or hang by your neck, your hands tied. Tie his hands, they did. Maybe our spirit guides could eat you. They are living to see how much blood you have. We could make bets and see. Take off his everything, foot ware to, have him stand like an animal be for us.

Moon Boy asks our spirit guides to kill him slow. No, no do not do it, then tell me what I would like to know, leave out nothing, if you do, the death whirl will begin if it starts no one can stop it. Cubby tell him how much you enjoy killing him, Cubby growled his terrible sound, his face a mask of rage the crow all most passed out, water ran from between his legs, not sweet he had soiled him self. Tall Elk asked, "How many? Ten plus, ten plus, ten, plus three more, and me." "And you? You are no more. You are dead, you have not told me truth," "yes I have". How is the chief called? Bent Feather the brother of Yellow Tail, who you killed in big fight. What big fight? No little fight it was almost over before it started, they died like rabbits.

The captive by now was so frightened he shuck like a young tree in a strong wind, he fell no longer able to stand. Let me be a Sioux, like Buffalo Tongue or Runs Fast or the others, I will be a good Sioux. What do you mean good Sioux? You would not make a good woman. You have no honor; I see why they sent you first to catch worms for them to eat at first light that's all you are good for. The brave could stand no more he jumped at Tall Elk, tied as he was. The chief hit him, he fell out cold. Now I think he will tell us.

All tie him by his feet and build a little fire under his head, high enough not to cock him or hurt him, but he will not know this. When the crow brave came to he was terrified, swinging by his feet over a fire they were going to cock him. I will tell you all, everything you want to know, lower him more I think he is not ready yet, and put more wood on he screamed loud. Take him down, now why do you keep coming to our hunting grounds we have killed most of you now. We want your spirit guides, your horse and your women. The chief hit him, stupid one, the spirit guides belong to themselves, our women would not spit on your dust and now you all will die, and your hair will blow in the wind at our lodge openings, you are to dumb to live and eat good buffalo, tie him hard no food or water.

Eagle floated in on spread wings sat down and said they are just waiting, looking this way. Some of them want to go back I think. They ride off and a big one talks to them, much waving of lances and arms then they come back, only to talk loud more some get on horse and go of a ways. Get eagle meat, and pack to then we should eat we will ride soon, I think. Fill your quivers with Skunks arrows tips, make sure your lance tips are set good get axe ready all so your knife. Eagle said I go to watch, if I come and scream they will be moving. Moon Boy ask the spirit guides to spook the horses, as before, they don't like arrows all at once so bow braves shot as before, we will see. Sun was not to mid point, when eagle came in, they are moving, ten and six of them are running back very fast, ten and seven are coming to this place. I go to watch, the spirit guides went west to look running spread out and fast.

Tall Elk and the braves, with Moon Boy on his bay, rode west. Ten then ten and ten more and then two more miles they rode. Moon Boy had his crow bow and his new arrows, father what should I do in the fight? Stay back you are to young to fight men, only if you have to shot to help one of us. Your part talk to our spirit guides make sure we know all, the captive ran with nothing on his feet were bloody from rocks and thorns, no one was sorry. Curly ran up to them, they come, all in a line. Tall Elk asked, "We need a draw to stake out the captive in, is one like that near by? Yes come I will show you," they came to the draw, up near the top Tall Elk gagged the captive and tied him. Go up there and get behind sage rocks and when they bunch around him, send your arrows fast then again, others go to each side shot as the ones in front. I and the ax and club braves will come fast, if the chief is not dead good, this time I want to take him to his camp in shame. I don't want him to come again to our county. "Curly when the arrows stop. Explode the horse, as before now get ready and wait for them".

The wait was not long, over the rise to the west a rider sat on his horse, then more, now a bunch of them sat all looked, no movement then they came all in a group up to the bound brave, one got down to free him. Arrows came from three sides, again and again braves down others wounded the pack hit the horses screaming plunging kicking and bucking. Tall Elk came charging from three sides with club and ax, Bent Feather was hit with three arrows was trying to rally his braves most were beyond his control and was on there way to happy hunting ground, their ears closed to him or any one else. Tall Elk hit Bent Feather with the club knocking him out tie him. One other crow was not killed tie him it was over. Horse Dancer or worm catcher, the scout was dead an arrow in his neck.

Fifteen enemies was dead two would live to remember that bad sun in Sioux draw, they came to a place they were not wanted or needed and paid the full price for their stupid act, now they were gone, the law was the law. Tall Elk was tired it had been a long sun, they were lucky only two Sioux were wounded, and not to bad. Spotted Owl and Runs Fast had knife cuts they were bandaged and given food and drink they rested.

The chief said get the horses and all of their war things, your arrows too, leave nothing, and get their feathers to and their hair. This time they will lie as they have fallen. You, Bent Feather will die at your camp in front of your people in shame, you killed your braves, and you should have stayed in your own country. One's that went back are far smarter then you are. Bent Feather looked puzzled, our spirit guides and eagle has watched you stupid one for three suns, and we know all. Tall Elk took the feathers from the chief hair, got his knife and cut his long hair off at the skull. Now you look more like the little boy you are. Your mother should take your skin off your butt, with a willow stick for killing your braves. Tall Elk tied the long hair to a long stick and put it in the ground for all to see it flutter in the breezes. Ho it looks better on the a stick, then on you, little boy with out hair Bent Feather was so enraged he forgot he was tied hand and foot and made a lunge at Tall Elk only to flop on the ground like a turkey with his head gone. All laughed. Bring the horses, they did.

Bent Feather had a splendid white stallion, tall and well proportioned. He moved like flowing water his, gate was smooth with no jolt at all. Tall Elk went to him and stroked his glossy coat, I take this horse. The stallion arched his proud neck and side stepped a little. He was so beautiful, one must look at him with eyes squinted to see him at all. Bent Feathers face was a mask of rage. He bit his lip so blood ran if you had stayed in your camp, and not come to kill us he would still be yours. You lost him little boy, with out hair because you were greedy and stupid. Nothing under this big sun will change that.

The others in the horse heard were good also, there were more horses then riders so they must have been going to take their dead back with them. Find a poor horse and put no hair on him looking back. Tie his feet; put the other on a good one.

He is enemies but not stupid. He will ride as a brave should ride. Let us go to camp and so they did leading a string of fine horses. The last sight that Bent Feather saw was his long braids waving in the breezes, he thought of his brother's son Bird Wings words. The Sioux are bad they have wolves helping them. The wolves talk to them, and the Sioux understand and talk back. Bent Feather had blue air though his nose and said bosh you lie. Wolves can't do that. But this sun he had seen it, and now he, Bent Feather was chief no more. His braves were dead, his white stallion was rode by this Sioux, who cut his hair off and put it on a stick to fly in the wind.

He wished he could die, rather then face the shame. He wished he could cry, but that he could not do. The horse he was on was old bad gated and thin. Only good for packing dead back to their county. Now he the chief was riding him looking back. He was hungry, thirsty, and sick and like Bird Wing he was done with the war trail. Not by choice but dead braves do not go on raids.

How far to their camp? The old horses back was cutting him in two like an ax cuts cotton wood in winter. His head hurt from the blow of the war club, and now the wolf pack was following him making the old horse skittish. It could not get worse, but it did. They went faster until every bone and joint hurt now he had to make water so he did. The water ran off the horse and on the ground, he was past caring.

One Skunk said to Looking Back Horse, "I am thinking why I should make so many bows, when the enemies keep giving us theirs. More then we can use that is what I was thinking." Looking Back Horse looked at Skunk and shook his head and smiled. That Skunk had a way with words. One Skunk was a friend of every one. When he told stories, as many as possible, would sit or stand came to hear. Many a laugh or chuckle was heard. He did not mean to be funny he just was. As with all things, good or bad it comes to an end some time, and some time was now.

Tall Elk rode in to camp, riding the white stallion, leading the black with white legs half way up. Moon Boy on his bay, with white fore legs. The bay was side stepping and acting up. It was quite a sight. Every one in camp were looking, no one was missing. A big cheer was sounded then all looked at the new horses, pinto's bays, cream colored, and many more different shades in between.

Then all looked at Bent Feather and knew he must be the crow chief, setting backwards on an old nag of a horse with his hair cut off.

Tall Elk got the lead rope of the old nag and rode around the camp. This was Bent Feather chief of the enemies, now he is called little boy with out hair, all laughed he spoke in sign talk so his captive would know, he is stupid, he killed the braves who rode with him, he rode for revenge, all he got for them was death. Now he will have death, but not soon for three suns he will have no food or drink. He will be tied to the post, every one can see him. If any woman has an old dress, we will put it on him. A dress was given to Tall Elk. But first Moon Boy do you see a horse you like? The boy picked a long leg roan mare for his pick. If any one likes a horse takes him, when done all horses had new owners.

Bent Feather was taken of the old horse his clothes were taken off and the dress put on him, he then was tied to the post. The other captive was taken to Tall Elk lodge and sat on the ground, to wait, Moon Boy, call our spirit guides he did ask Curly if they are alright? They were. Get food for them and then ask them to watch the one tied at the post, if he tries to free himself tell us. Now we will eat, give food and water to the captive, it was done. After all had been feed Tall Elk raised his arms and asked the braves to come to smoke, when the pipes were going the chief asked the captive. "How are you called the captive made sign to his tied hands his hands were untied." I am called Drinks Plenty, why did you come on your raid? I wanted to take horses to give to Old Bull for a wife, he has many girls.

I would have given captured horses for a wife, old chief said it would be easy, that you were week and afraid to get far from your women skirt. Is that why you rode off and he told you to ride with him?" "Yes, you were lucky you should be out in draw with the rest of them I know, Buffalo Tongue, Runs Fast, and Bull Tail do you know him? Yes we know him, Drinks plenty if I let you live, will you be a Sioux? You will learn our ways and fight with us even against others of your kind. It seems they can not get enough of dying from us. If our Sioux braves say yes and then you may live, and be one of us.

The three spoke a short time and said we told him should he not do as he said he would we would kill him fast, and that would be all. Bent Feather screamed, "Old women you will not ride with me again, that is right you walk when you go to die or ride backwards on that old horse you like so well, we will starve him so he better to ride." How do you get along with our spirit guides? Be of good talk with them may be they will kill you faster. Bent Feather was very uncomfortable.

He screamed out something in crow the new Sioux said, meet me in combat you son of a snake I will kill you with my teeth, I will kill you with my feet, you are afraid to meet me. All the braves have left me. I am alone, so fight me if you dare. Tall Elk went to him, I could kill you fast but we lost six good braves the last time your braves came and you will think long on it. We lost a boy doing braves work, because of that your people lost many more and gained nothing. Not one horse did they get, now think on it. I see some hair growing back may be you need your hair cut more the chief started to go then felt pity he turned and held the water skin to his mouth and let him drink. Bent Feather was shaking from the cold water but he felt better. Watch him Curly so he don't get free the wolf nodded this understanding.

When sun came back One Skunk brought a new bow for the chief to look at, I have been working on this. It will send an arrow faster and longer then others; see it is curved more and smaller at the ends that give it more power. Also it has horn strips to give it more power it is a chiefs bow I give it to you, Tall Elk thank you, my brother I will use it well in the hunt and in battle. I made one for me too and I will make one for your son when he is older.

One Skunk said I was thinking, may be some one could go with to find grand father real snake. I need more of his poison. I would go this sun may be if some one could come and help me find him he hides well. How many do you need to go may, be ten or how many can go. Good I will ask some to go, this sun he got up went in his lodge he come back with some stew. Eat this, my wife cooks good, the Skunk did. Tall Elk cleared his wind pip, "my brothers, Skunk would go look for the real snake, he needs to borrow some of his poison he asks that some of us go and help find snake he hides good. He would like ten or more to go with him."

When sun was two hands high Skunk and ten and fore braves went to find snake, the new Sioux Drinks Plenty was one of the ones going all so Buffalo Tongue and Runs Fast each had a long stick, with a forked end to hold snakes head. So you could get a hold of snake, One Skunk had a little bag to put the poison in; he knew how to get snake to spit the poison in bag.

When sun was midpoint thirty or more snakes had give poison to Skunk, now we are ready for more war said Skunk. One Skunk came in with his helpers, all were in good humor. It had been easy to do some think it would be very dangerous they were in the best humor. No one had been hurt at all. At the post Bent Feather screamed, "Sioux dogs, sons of snakes you would help them, while I your chief am tied, with no food or water?

Buffalo Tongue walked over to the post, and spat at him you, are chief no longer to me, or any of us. You are so filled with hate it run out your mouth, you would not hear Bird Wing, he told you not to go on this war trail, and now crow women are by them selves, because of you, young boys have no fathers to show them how to hunt, You are bad I will go to see you die, I hope the spirit guides take a long time killing you." Bent Feather was stunned, "the wolves? No not the wolves," he thought combat to die bravely, a chance to kill Tall Elk, but wolves he had feared wolves all his life. He was getting sick, his legs felt weak he was passing out, not wolves.

Tall Elk found him slumped at the post, he splashed water on him, when the crow regained his senses, he said not wolves, don't kill me with wolves. I fear wolves. Untie him and let his blood move in him, he has been tied three suns, Bent Feather fell, and he could not stand. Walk him some so he can eat they did. Now drink and eat, when sun comes again we take you back to your county. On a hill near your camp so all can see you die. Go get the old horse, so they can see each other, they travel on next sun for last time, it was done. Tie him. Moon Boy call our spirit guides, they were there, tell them what we would do on next sun he did. Curly nodded, good Cubby went to the captive lifted his lips and out came his terrible growl Bent Feathers face went white, he past out, coward all said.

Tall Elk was on the white stallion. He had his new bow and many arrows, his club and ax, Moon Boy had his bow and his new arrows on the bay, all rode good horse. They put No Hair on the old nag backwards, tied his feet took off the women dress, he rode with nothing on. The spirit guides were on two sides and back. Forty braves and one very sad captive rode west, eagle glided on air currants far above watching.

By the time they past the fight site, no hair was sick. He saw his long hair fluttering in the breeze on the stick, his belly tuned over. He spilled all he ate on the old horse's hind quarters. It was a long way to his camp and he wished he had never thought of coming. Too late, he was so proud. He should have heard the words of his dead brother's son, Bird Wing. In fact he should hear his wife's words and she told him not to go. Now he was coming back, but not like he wanted to, the wolves lopping on all sides of him looking up at him and it seemed they were smiling as they ran, just waiting to kill him.

The air was so sweet with blooms and grass growing. Why did he have to be so stupid! He had it all. Now he had nothing? If Tall Elk let him go, he knew in a short time, he would do it again his pride would not let him rest. The long line of Sioux was painted for war, with feathers and plums flying in the wind. Lance tip gleaming in the sun, the horses prancing a sight to strike fear to any enemies camp, and he naked on an old horse backwards. Soon it would be past. They were nearing the camp of the crow. They had rode one sun and part of that night.

Now with sun at mid point his hill was in front of him. Now they were there, Tall Elk put them in a long line. Two Sioux Crow rode down the hill to talk to the camp. Two Crow came out to talk, Buffalo Tongue and Bull Tail. He told them this not a raid, they had not come to kill crow. To many had died all ready. The crow said then why did you come? We brought Bent Feather back to kill him in front of all, many crow are dead in our country because of him, and some of us too. If we turn him free he will come again we are tired of him coming. How will he die? Our spirit guides will kill him. We will turn him free, and then the wolves will do the rest. Do not try to help him, or some of you may die.

The crow went back to camp. Soon they were back and we will not help him. When it is done, we will put him in a tree. Moon Boy said to the pack. Kill him slow, but kill him Tall Elk and two other Sioux took no hair of the old nag. The chief said now you will never bother us more. You are bad, you killed for no reason. I kill you for good reason. Let me live I will not come again. Tall Elk looked a long time at him then said. "Take him down the hill a short way." They did. The she wolf said. "Circle him fast, make no sound then Cubby you do your sound. Then you on his back side cut him some.

Just a little the circle was started." Cubby growled. No hair leaped up he tried to run they cut him of Curly cut his legs no hair screamed and fell Fatty slashed his arm blood was running they cut his back sides and but at the same time no hair grabbed Sniff by the tail and hung on mother broke his arm, his scream was so loud it could be heard a long way of Dusty Rose cut his belly open, so his insides came out. He got to his feet. They cut his tendons again he screamed but weaker now. Mother cut his throat.

The pack came back to set by Moon Boy, who patted their necks. Tall Elk pointed at two Sioux Crow get his horse. Take the rope of the nag and put the body of no hair on it. Then take him to the waiting crow. Now it is done. If you have wife and wants to come with us she and family are welcome. All Sioux Crow family is welcome. We will wait for them to get ready.

All the Sioux braves had some one so they got started. Down came lodges bags packed horses got in to pull and ride. Now may be we will have no more wars. The old crow chief said, "Yes Tall Elk nodded. Now we have no more wars, it is good."

When all was ready, Tall Elk pointed east, "let us go," so they did. The travel was slower now. The lodges could not move as fast as horsemen could, but the pull horses were fresh and moved at a trot in most places. Slowing down only when the ground was rocky or steep. Shadows pointed east and were growing longer as the sun got lower in the west. To the north east a bunch of buffalo were grazing on the flat. Tall Elk pointed and said, "Go kill two so we can have hump ribs. Some braves cut of the column and lopped off before the sun fell of the western edge. They found a spring of good sweet water and made fast camp, built fires.

When this was finished the braves brought meat in. Soon buffalo was cooking, sizzling over the fires. The wife's and girl are doing most of the cooking. A few braves, beat grass and brush, making sure no real snakes were around. The women cleaned and scraped the hides. Some would need bigger lodges. At first light, some meat was cooked and eaten. Horses were loaded others hitched to the lodge drags.

Tall Elk sat on his white stallion. Moon Boy on the bay with white for legs, sat next to him. The spirit guides lounged near by. When all was ready the chief turned east, and they all followed, the march had begin. The pace was brisk when sun was at midpoint they watered at a stream. Let the horses graze a little. They ate meat from last night's camp, mounted and were gone. Just before sun down Tall Elk stopped the column and made a quick camp. The horses needed rest, fires was lighted. Six Sioux had went hunting Moon Boy went also. They were back now, with five antelope. A real treat! The women skinned them and dressed the skins out. There would be enough for two dresses when finished.

Moon Boy sat by his father, I asked our spirit guides to bring them to us, they did. When the antelope were close we all shot arrows fast. I did too. One of my arrows hit one, very good, my son. I am proud of you. The pack ate some to. Good they got them near and you should have given them some. I gave them liver and heart from the one I shot, and other parts they like, good said the chief, I will make you sub chief soon. Then I can rest all sun and watch.

Moon Boy was pleased with his father's words. Even if he knew his father was just trying to make him feel good. He Moon Boy had been on three war raids, and he just seven summers old. He knew he was to talk to the spirit guides and that was the only reason he was along, but he was there, and had seen braves die.

He, Moon Boy had his own bow and quiver, with arrows. One Skunk, had made for him, and had killed a deer, and now an antelope he felt good. No other boy had done so much, his age and he, Moon Boy with a sight problem. He hoped, maybe to see better sometime. As long as he had Curly and Cubby with him, he saw with their eyes and heard with their ears. He could not smell with their nose yet but may be that to, would come. After he ate the very good meat he got the robe he sat on all sun. On the bay curled up and was soon asleep, with Curly on his right, and Cubby on his left with the two wolves watching over him. Nothing could bother him. Sun had again colored the east with a pink glow. Soon full light would be, here it was time to go. So they did.

Chapter Nine

By mid sun they were at the last kill place. The hair of Bent Feather still floated on the stick, the air moving it gently back and forth. The rest of the scene was horrible to look at. The dead lay in every position you could thing of. The lesser meat eaters had been there tearing at the bodies of all the dead, all bloated and discolored. The smell would gag a maggot.

All looked the other way, no one wanted to see, it was bad. When sun was at high point, the long line of braves entered camp. The camp crier helped show the new lodges places to set. War gear was put away, and horses rubbed down and turned to grass. Tall Elk and Moon Boy went to their lodge, packing their gear. They hung the war things up and sat down. Glad to be back it had been a long ride.

Sweet Grass and Dove Tail had food ready so they ate. Good, it was very good. It was good to sit down and not on a horse. Has any thing happened when we were gone? May Flower was setting on her fathers leg, showing him her doll. See father my doll has flowers in her hair pretty? Yes very pretty. Dove Tail smiled at Tall Elk, "You will be father again when snow is deep. You will have to hunt more and we will get more herbs and berries to make stew taste better." "Yes it will be good. I just hope my new son is as good as Moon Boy is. He is good with his bow and getting better he killed an antelope on the run with one arrow, and it was a braves bow, but he can pull it. Anything more that happened?" "The braves were with you, all the women did camp chores, and watched for you and the braves. Old grand father real snake come we chased him out of camp." Tall Elk said. "I think we are done with war."

With that crow band, we killed most of the fighting braves, just say spirit guides to them and they are gone, but there other bands we must watch. Moon Boy call our spirit guides, they came, ask Curly to scout. Some other bands may still come and want horse or us. Curly you and the pack go south a long way, then swing west then north. If you find any new sign or braves moving, come back fast. We will move the camp east, down river to better grass, or we may wait for you to return.

Curly understood all. Are you hungry? The packs got up and ran south and were gone. Tall Elk asked his son to get the crier, he came, ask Iron People, Taken Alive, One Skunk, Looking Back Horse, Yellow Footed Dog, Runs Fast, Bears Tail and maybe more to come to my lodge. We will plan, Moon Boy get the white stallion and your bay. Put pad on them, get your bow and mine. Also get our knives.

When all were there, Tall Elk said, "My brothers we have stepped over and around dung long enough. Get your horses and bows let us go down river and find a place to move camp. When all were ready they mounted and rode east down river. They were looking for a place were water ran over rocks, with a stand of timber, that had tall young cotton woods, all need new lodge polls, and I think a new lodge or two may be needed soon. They found such a spot were the river made a bend water did run over ripples. A thick stand of timber grew by the waters edge, only to spread out to a few tall giant cotton woods that were good for shade.

Ho, we have found the good place put camp. They had brought extra horses; let us find some buffalo for evening fires, Ho all said, let us do it, so they did. They rode up on the flat and of to the right some buffalo were trailing to water. Some cows with last year's calves and this year are to. They did not look at the Sioux, all pulled their bows and let fly. All fell but the one. Moon Boy hit it. He took two arrows for that one; all the braves begin to skin out their kills even Moon Boy started skinning out his. He pulled out the arrows cleaned them and put them away. He had hind quarters skinned and was working on the belly when Skunk came. Ho, let me help you I am hungry for hump ribs from this one and I would eat before next sun. The meat was loaded and they all went to camp. Fires were lighted soon the meat was good smelling. Hides were paged out the scrapping started. Tall Elk said in three suns we go to new camp, so start packing.

The she wolf took them south in a straight line, then turned a little west then south again. All spread out covering more ground. They crossed horse tracks, wild horses no man sent. They turned a little west and ran to the next water shed, watered and ran the banks they found nothing. Curly barked a short sound, and took the lead. He smelled some thing or, thought he did. He took them south again up a wide draw, with ash trees. In a clearing to one side was a kill, a mule deer lay there only eaten a little of. Curly and the others circled and sniffed the deer, their nose reading it like a page from a book. Three wolves had killed the deer, and was still near. Curly tore of piece of warm meat and ate it as did Cubby. Soon they all did, Curly looked up and saw a little she wolf watching them he walked over and touched noses, he said come and eat with us it is your kill, so she did. My name is Curly, the others are my family my mother brothers and sisters, We help a band of man things. Someone are always trying to kill them, so we watch and scout for them, and they have a little one who does not see well. I and Cubby take care of him, you could help. I am Blue Dawn; I will run with you Curly and be friends with all the rest, good now that is settled. Who are the other two? An old he wolf, he don't talk much, he is cross and bad tempered we leave him be, the other is clumsy. I do the killing of game, now he will, or go hungry. Curly said, "I run at mothers right, now you run at my right let us go so they did. Blue Dawn had a good nose she got wind of the camp first, they spread out, and looked at the camp a peace full camp. The she wolf said, "go way a round them they mean us no harm or our band."

When sun was at three paws past mid point they saw eagle she floated down and she and the she wolf talked long. Out to the west, the crow are very angry. Not the band of Bent Feather but he has relatives and friends in other bands of crow. They say the sioux should be punished for killing a chief in sight of the camp, and no one doing nothing about it. Some of them plan a war but so far they can not find enough braves to go against. Your spirit guides and me, and eagle laughed. All thought it was funny not one of them could pull a bow, but not any of them could fly either or run to fast to see. Now there was one more spirit guide, bad luck for the enemies. Go north from here, there is nothing west yet go tell Tall Elk he must be ready for them. They will come from two ways I think. A small group, head on and the bigger group on his back side. If the crow fail this time, Moon Boy will be chief next time, they try. It will be year's maybe. Maybe we could talk them out of war? How we can only talk to Moon Boy and no crow would hear him. We now have two more eagles that now fly with us; we can now take turns watching. That's good, maybe we could have a flying war party, all laughed. Fatty said if eagle had ten of his brother's help, each had a big rock. They could drop the rocks on their heads of the enemies they may go back, eagle looked wise it may work. But you should go wolves. Tall Elk needs to know what the Crow are thinking. The she wolf took them north at that long swinging lope, that made long distances seam like nothing.

Just as moon was falling of the west side of the world, the pack was at Tall Elks lodge. Curly and Cubby gave the short bark sound and the chief and son was out and was hearing. We saw eagle many miles west. The Crow are very angry. Not Bent Feathers band but other crow bands. They are planning a big war. They lacking two things, one they have no strong leader yet and brave's to follow and all are afraid of us and eagle. Now we have two more eagles and one more spirit guide, see here she is. Curly said, "This is Blue Dawn, she will be my mate when we are ready." Moon Boy got to his knees, as did Tall Elk. You are welcome she nodded her understanding. This is the one we take care of, we see for him. Eagle thinks they will come from two ways, a small group will hit you head on, the other bigger group will come from the back side if they fail they will not come again. They know that they can not sneak up so they will come at mid sun or more. I don't think they will come at first sun but we must be ready. We must plan. I would speak with One Skunk go get him.

One Skunk was there. Ho our spirit guides are up with the birds. Yes we have been talking with a bird, an eagle. She has been watching the crow. They are planning a big war, but no braves want to go on it yet and no chief wants to lead because of spirit guides, and eagle they are afraid. But eagle said, "be ready. If we fight with a high cut bank behind us they will not be able to come that way and if you, Skunk put your drop of snake poison on arrow point, that will help. Can you make more bows like the one you made for Tall Elk? Good, ten bows could send ten arrows fast, then ten more fast, before they could shot one." One Skunk said, "I will start now." Tall Elk asked, "Who do you want to help you? Looking Back Horse, Spotted Owl, Runs Fast and Iron People are all good." "Have Yellow Footed Dog and Bears Tail look at our crow bows see they are set right, ours too." Tall Elk said, "The new camp has the big cut bank around on three sides, we should go now and we can work over there on fresh ground, no dung to step in." Horses were got in and hocked up bundled packed and for dragging with so many working it did not take long. The rest of the horses come along like dogs.

Soon they were at the camp sight lodges sprang up like magic, back far enough so no arrow could be shot of rim. All lodges openings were on the south east so sun could come each morning, and warm them. The camp people were asked to place dung in one general spot and cover with sand if they could, to avoid a mess. In the timber much old logs lay. Tall Elk said, "Pull old logs we won't burn and make a fence. If the crow come off the hill they can not get behind us do it on two sides. Moon Boy sat on his bay, the pack was with him. His bow and quiver on his back, he had a rope of raw hide and his knife.

He rode up along the rim to see all the activity. Braves were getting thing in order in camp making sure all was as it should be. The pack was looking west then south nothing yet no word from eagle. It was too early then his father was there on his big black with white half way up legs. I wish you would tell us when you ride my son. In this sun enemies are coming, you should be careful, and the spirit guides we need them bad on the west edge of camp. So they rode back to camp, to the west side and on to the old camp, and saw nothing.

Curley said, "I think eagle is coming, a dot then another two eagles was coming. She sat on the stump the others near her, they are trying to get braves to come, they will come but few of them when they start we will tell you. Go as before, kill them and I think it will be all. Ask eagle how many do you think are coming? I do not know. We will know when they start. One of us was setting in a tree at the crow camp; the crows said it would be Beavers Tail that would lead the crow. He is a son of the last chief brother, so he feels angry at the Sioux; he also fears our spirit guides and eagle. Now what one will he obey?

His fear or his anger? I don't know, either way he will be a weak chief. Before you go are you hungry? No, we ate not long ago. Eagle how far is it to the crow camp? Two or three suns, if you go fast. Pick the best horse for the job and practice a lot. Run him through the job over, many times. Have shooting contests it is good and keeps your mind of the war, but gets you ready for it at the same time. Cook food a head time. That's one less thing you have to do. Don't get to jumpy, when you hear them scream. That's what they want you do. Moon Boy asked his father, how eagle got so wise on war. You should ask him, next time you see him, when someone is helping you, who don't have to and you can see it is good. Do not insult him with a lot of questions that are obvious to every one to see. Eagles flew away, and Tall Elk and sun went back to camp.

The chief said hear me my brothers. Get the new bows and some practice arrows, One Skunk, hold up your best one, and show it to us. He did. Set up targets far farther and real far. Skunk put an arrow to the string, pulled; twang the arrow went so fast you could barely track it and hit the target. Ho it was the one real far. I made ten like this. Tall Elk has one, I have one and ten of our very best bow shots should have one now. Come let's shoot and see who is best. You good arrow makers go make arrows then I will put poison on tips. We will see, almost every one came to see the arrows fly. It was good, all felt better, they were proud to see all the hits and not many miss. At the end of the shooting ten new bows, were in the hands of the best.

One Skunk and his helpers had gone to ash and oak trees to get more wood. Had the crow seen this they would have broke theirs, and stayed in camp, for at the time the bows of One Skunk were made. They was the best in the world, anywhere. It is so sad, but true, the best man kind, can do is oft tangled with their bones, and remembered no more. But I can, and now you can too.

One Skunk and his helpers brought back good wood, boiled much buffalo horn, cut it in strips to be glued on bows. Bows were shaped and scraped for thickness and length and balance and if ten of these arrows were shot at you, at the same time, you had better be on a tall horse, with a head start. Tall Elk said, "Now my brothers get the horse you will ride in the fight, bring him in and explain to him, how important it is, to work well together with others of the band. We take care of the horse, and in battle the horse must take care of you. Go get the horse you will use, then we will see." So they did.

Tall Elk got his black stallion with white for legs half way up, with the white star. Moon Boy chose the bay with white for legs. He would not be in the battle but he would talk with the spirit guides, and have his crow bow and quiver with Skunks arrows. All the braves had their horse; they would ride and had talked it over with the horse. What he would do in this case or that and it was amazing what a difference, it made between horse and rider.

They could mount sixty six braves for battle but would leave fifteen braves back to help defend the camp. Tall Elk said to the women, boys, and older ones cook food. Make thing ready to fix cut and arrow pokes, we will need you to. All were ready, and every one was nervous. It would be better once it got started then every brave would know what to do, as in most cases the waiting is harder then the doing.

The pack was on edge to. Curly came and sat down by Moon Boy. Mother said, "We should go run a little and see what can be seen. Just sitting is not good for us we need to be moving. Tall Elk thought it would be good so the pack was gone off looking. Every nerve ending, tingling and alive yet eyes looking far and close. Noses reading air currents up and down the land. Yet not finding anything that could be called enemies. Eagle gliding, sat on a rock near Moon Boy went to her. Eagle looked at the boy. Tell your father, some are coming, not fast, no dancing, no drums, no jumping over fire, just coming.

Tall Elk said, "A war trail that starts of dead, soon are. Beaver Tail has only four braves with him, just four and he rides like he must put one foot down. Then go find a spot to put one more." The second eagle came in and talked to the first, more are coming from other camps now. There are six, from one camp and two and five from another camp. One camp are sending ten braves, but they ride like they have lost the war and are going back to camp to try to explain why. When will they all come together? Tall Elk asked. Eagle said the first five are not that far, may be one sun, if you ride fast. Tall Elk asked, "What is your thoughts my, brothers, Looking Back Horse and Taken Alive said our words are to go catch the first five, leave sign and bring them to our camp. When the others get there, we will talk.

If they agree to go and not bother us more, we will have no war and then we can see. Good Tall Elk said thirty of you get ready to go now.

Moon Boy and the spirit guides and the two eagles were out in front the rest rode fast behind. All that sun they rode, and into the night. Moon Boy came back, they are camped. The pack has them. They circled the crow and were all around them. You are caught, do not move or you die. Get the horse and tie them on get their war things. Now let us go. They did they were told. Back in camp the next night, tie them to the poles. All the Sioux and their helpers ate. It had been along sun, bring food and drink to our captives. Untie their hands so we can talk and eat. Now Beaver Tail why are you here? To have revenge for all the things you did to us. Are you having revenge now? No, you look smarter then Bent Feather. Do you want to die as he did? You mean the spirit guides? "Yes." No, no never that. Then you must give up your plan for revenge, all of it. The ones coming must give up to. We killed Bent Feather because he was evil. He was bad and would not change. I don't see that in you, we could be friends, you and I or we could kill you, and if we do the spirit guides will do it.

Show me his bow. One Skunk had it. Tall Elk looked at it. The bow was massive, he tried the pull a little more then his. Skunk asked who your bow maker is, Looking Eagle I am here is that cider wood? Yes that is good the Skunk said I want to try some soon, I am One Skunk, I am bow maker for this band of Sioux. Here look at mine it is ash wood with horn strips glued on, to give it power. I do that also Looking Eagle said. Good I hope we don't have to kill you, I also. What are you three called? I am Tall Moon. I am Walks Big, I am Long Bull. By the way you were coming slowly and with out much energy, I think you did not want to come very bad. How did you know that? Eagles were watching you come and our wolves watched you we know all things that are why you can never catch us napping. And when the first ones came our spirit guides saw you and came and got Tall Elk and we caught them in their robes.

Moon Boy is our chief's son and the spirit guides have pledged to help him. He doesn't see well, so they see for him, they can talk to him, and he to them. When he rides his horse he sees both sides of the ridge at the same time and in front and back to. No one has ever done this before.

Three eagles watch from the air very high so Moon Boy is safe, but our enemies are not. Eagle glided in and sat near Moon Boy. She told him to tell his father the others had just got to the place was the five braves were caught, and all was confusion. "What did she say?" Looking Eagle asked. She said the rest of the braves are now at the place we got you five she will go back so one of the others can come and report. Moon Boy call our spirit guides they were there, that fast? How can it be, they were not in sight, then they were standing, sitting, and laying all around Moon Boy and he patting, rubbing and making over them. Are you hungry? Curly licked his lips and smiled. Get food for them we may soon have to go kill more of Looking Eagles people.

Tall Elk said. "Moon Boy ask our spirit guides to go back to mid point if they come send someone fast so we can meat them. Call an eagle. A dark spot formed to the west, got bigger as it got closer. Now you could make out an eagle was coming. Then she was there she circled once and sat down by Moon Boy. Eagle laughed; tell your father that every sound the new braves heard they would jump around like eaglets in a nest. Then someone else would move and they would jump around again. Then I flew over head and screamed and they jumped so fast that they jumped into each other. Some fell down. You should have been there.

They are talking among themselves and watching the east. If you had only one brave and appeared upon the hill to the east I think they go back. Everyone laughed. Tall Elk asked Eagle, "How many are there now" ten and ten and one. Tall Elk said, "Forty of you get fresh horses and Moon Boys, tall roan mare and let's go chase them home. The rest of you stay in camp. When we get back we will talk more on cedar bows. Get your bow and quivers, your ax and lance lets go fast. We will pick up the spirit guides on the way", and so they did. In a short time they were with the pack. They settled into a faster pace.

The sun was casting long shadows to the east and then they were there. The spirit guides circled the twenty one frightened braves. Buffalo Tongue yelled out in good crow, "Stop you are caught. Get off horse and now sit on the ground in front of horse. Do not move". Tall Elk said, "Tie them and put them on their horses. Now lets us go back to camp". The captives kept watching the spirit guides. Soon they were all headed back to the Sioux camp. They moved at a leisurely pace, they were not fresh. As sun brought his torch back to the east they were at camp. Turn the horses loose and tie the captives. When the sun is higher and we have slept a little longer we will decide what to do with them.

When sun was at mid point, Tall Elk came out of his lodge, let us eat get food for the captives, it was done. Five times you crow people have came to our country, to kill, take horse and take captive. You have not got one horse, not one captive, you did kill six of us, but many of you are in trees some on the ground. No good has come out of your raids; you lost very good horse I ride two of your best. Of the last braves we will see, I don't think I will want any of you. When you were caught you were too afraid to help yourself the Sioux have no cowards. May be you will grow out of it but do it some place else. If you should come back you will die by our spirit guides and us. You twenty one come and stand in front of me, I want to see face, not your names.

They lined up and Tall Elk looked long at them, I know you now take of every thing they did get them five older bows and for arrows for each bow, get ten and one very old horse and one knife for cutting. Say nothing as you ride away or I will kill you. Then you are lucky to ride. I meant to give you to our wolves to kill I still may. The old nags were standing, heads dropping. Now go they got up two to a horse and walked away, no one looked back. Looking Eagle, Walks Tall and Long Bull and I, Tall Elk would ask you to stay with us and be one of us, if you will. You Beaver Tail and Tall Moon you must go back to your country. We will give you a good horse, and some thing to kill meat with and a knife to cut. I would keep you, but you are needed in your camps I think. Get two horses and two bows and four arrows each. Think no more of revenge all that is past. The two crows got on their horse and turned to go.

Call eagles they came watch and see they go if they turn around we will come and the sight we leave no one will for get, I have spoken. Do you need food or water Tall Elk? asked Looking Eagle and the other two? No not for a time I would have you show us how to make better bows. Skunk can make good bows very good, but the one I kept from Beaver Tail has a feel to it I like.

You kept his bow? Yes not good, he liked that bow. Bent Feather liked his white stallion also, but he came to our country and tried to kill me, and we killed him. The same with Turning Rock, I have his horse, now I have Beaver Tails bow. If they had stayed in their country they would have the things they liked. Now I say to you again, will you join us and be Sioux? Or will you want to stay crow? You can't have it two ways. Looking Eagle said, "I will be Sioux," The other two said we have wife and family in crow camp. We would like to get them. Tall Elk said they are well come as Sioux.

When the time is right we will get them. Now only Sioux live here. Ground was wet, resent rains had fallen and spring time was here, a lush green covered the land, spring flowers bloomed everywhere, the sweet aroma was intoxicating , gentle breezes came and went life was good. Young braves plaid the flute in front of girl's father's lodges, and horses were tied to lodge poles if enough horses were there, the father took them out to graze and new lodge poles were cut, many times the young brave moved in with the girl's family until enough buffalo skins could be gotten and tanned to make lodge covers. Old bull buffalo was much looked for because of his size, it took fewer skins to make a cover and if you boiled the meat long enough it lost the feel of old leather.

Moon Boy ask some young boys to hunt with you call our spirit guides he did, they were there, is eagle close? Yes Eagle did the crow get back to their country? Most of them did, some could not go back with nothing on and was unlucky. Real snake got him, one is making new bow and not happy Looking Eagle is with us he can not make the bow work well. Tall Elk asked the spirit guides to go with Moon Boy to hunt deer, antelope and Eagle too in case they need help fast. I would ask Skunk to go to, if he wants to. No just boys this time. I will ask Fat Leg and Frog to go good go then. Moon Boy got his bay and two horses for packing, his bow his quiver knife and robe and Sweet Grass gave him food and water skin.

They rode west past mule deer draw up over the hill and on the flats were antelope could be seen grazing. Moon Boy got his stick put a white skin on it put it in the ground, and all got their bows and waited for the antelope to come. Curiosity, would be antelopes undoing if he seen something he could not identify.

He could not rest until he figured out what was bothering him. Buck antelope saw the white thing fluttering on the crest of the rise, what was it? Two others were watching it did nothing, just moved a little in the wind. First antelope jumped made snorting sounds stomped sideways, nothing. The white thing was not afraid, it just stood there, the other two bucks pranced forward and looked they came very near, nothing no movement only a little flutter.

First antelope was mad, he would make it move, and he forgot the law. He would stomp it, he was looking down on it, he never saw the boys and only felt the arrows a little, the other two were down to all dead because they for got the law, they were careless. Moon Boy and the others took out the insides Curly and the pack ate them. Eagle got a heart. Moon Boy got the horses and the boys tied the antelope on, they would hurry it was warm and meat don't last long, before spoiling. They wiped the arrows on grass, mounted and lopped for camp; the horses were young and well feed they wanted to run. The trip seemed short back to camp. Ho Tall Elk said, you have done well, my son, he began to skin the antelope.

Sweet Grass and Doves Tail said let us do that, you may tear the skin, and we want a new dress. Tall Elk sat cross legged ,now tell me how you did this thing, Moon Boy told how he had put the stick with skin on top in the ground and just waited for antelope to come when they did, the boys put arrows in them fast, how did you know this? Buffalo Tongue told me that is how he did when he was ten, his grand father told him. Fat Legs and Frog go get your family we will eat this good meat, get Buffalo Tongue to.

When all had ate, Tall Elk said our boy have done well, when sun comes again, you Moon Boy and Fat Legs and Frog find three other boys around ten summers, ask One Skunk to see me, Skunk came I am asking nine boys to go with Moon Boy to the Grand River to the north, I would ask you to go to. Also ask Yellow Footed Dog to go, may be you can find some trees you like to make bows out of, the spirit guides will go also and Eagle. Skunk was showing all his teeth. It would be a good sun.

Moon Boy show me your arrows, Tall Elk put more arrows in the quiver. It is better to have more arrows and not need them, then have to few, and need them. Take pack horses, you may find some thing to bring back, take knife and ax to, and rope. One Skunk will go too also, Call our spirit guides and Eagle. Curly and Cubby be with Moon Boy. One on his right and one on his left, two in front, the rest in back, and eagle will be over you. Nothing can sneak up on you get ready go at first light. The bay was standing ready to go. The others horses were looked at three Tall Elk changed for better mounts, some of the boys had no bows they were given bows and quivers. Keep track of your arrows if you shoot pick it up, arrows don't grow on trees, and the boys that did have bows were given arrows, if they needed more. Go find game help Skunk, and he may be make a better bow for you. Moon Boy moved out and took the lead at the lope Curly on his right Cubby on his left Ling Lang and Dusty Rose up front, the rest fanned out behind Eagle overhead an unbeatable team.

Out over the ridge they swept, thunder rolling out from under their hooves. A sound that would make any one look Skunk moved up beside Moon Boy. Ho we need to slow down a little or I will have to run and let my horse ride me, all smiled Skunk backed the pace down to a long trot then to a fast walk, now look and see may be we can see game sign. Horse tracks, old but there plain in the mud, wild horse I think, not sure. Look good we should see them again, look to see the pattern if it changed we may have enemies in our country, or other riders we need to know. Over the hill a stream wandered, pull in I will look, Skunk got down he went and looked by the water, track go on they are ridden horse. Eagle sat down by Moon Boy ask eagle to look, he did. Eagle went north and was gone out of sight Moon Boy took them to the stream all watered let us eat some meat and see. What eagle finds out, he asked the pack to be ready also?

The boys dismounted and let the horses graze soon eagle was coming, she sat down and told Moon Boy, a small band of Sioux were camped on the next water, they were moving camp and would be gone when they got there. Moon Boy told them all, and eagle said much buffalo was there also and some elk, good all said. They mounted and crossed the stream, it was deep and cold they rode at a lope, soon buffalo were every where out in front and on two sides.

Moon Boy asked Skunk if they should kill one. No said Skunk not yet, they were on a ridge and could see the river brakes. An hour later they were looking at the Grand River, in a wide bottom, with much timber ash, oak and cedar good said Skunk hard wood for bows. Skunk said make little brush shelters Moon Boy get your bow let us have elk to eat they got down and looked over a bank a young bull elk stood in the willows two strings twanged and the bull fell. "Good I need his horns", Skunk asked the boy to get the older braves to help get him to camp. Soon the bull was skinned, fires crackled and a meal was cooked and cooked again. They could not get enough of the elk, the spirit guides and eagle all ate. Skunk pegged out the hide scrapped it put the horns in and rolled it for loading. Moon Boy got his robe rolled in it with Curly on his right, Cubby on his left, the other wolves all around him, and slept.

Moon Boy doesn't see well but has learned to shoot well with a chief's bow with the help of our spirit guides, you do see well. So you must learn to shoot starting now. All of you who had no bow get them. Skunk made some targets. Now put the arrow to the bow string and pull it back. Look down the arrow, snap the string and let fly they did. Now go look, out of four only one hit the target. Moon Boy get three arrows shot fast. All watch he did all arrows hit, get your arrows all did. I will make brave bows for you who learn to shot well. Get horse, let us go to trees, to find bow wood, so they did.

Sun was at mid point when they got back to camp. Skunk had ash, oak and cedar wood. When I make bows, I make them for brave's not little boy's bows. Touches The Wind you are the poorest shot of all the young braves but you have a good name, you must live up to it now. I am going to make you a brave bow you must learn to use it with honor. I One Skunk have spoken. Make fires and roast the rest of the elk, we will eat, then we will go up river then we will see. All ate and the elk was no more the spirit guides and eagle also ate. Skunk let them rest a little, then loaded up the bow wood and road west up river.

The Grand River wound along like a snake with to much wild grape wine to drink. Yellow Footed Dog found an out cropping of white flint. Perfect for arrow points, knifes and lance heads. They stayed until dark getting as much as possible. Moon Boy said, "We should make camp and may be come back when sun brings his torch back and may be find more flint. Our stone breaker will be very pleased". Ho all said. That is what we should do. They went and made camp, on the way a white tail deer was to slow.

Yellow Footed Dog put an arrow behind his left front leg. He was very good to eat. When the fires were just coals all were sleeping. Skunk was working on the bow he was making for Touches The Wind. He was all most done will it. It was long, tapered, graceful, and strong a bow any brave would want. Now you are a Sioux brave. Go use it well, I give it to you. You could not see Touches The Winds face all you could see was teeth. Thank you my brother I will use it well.

When sun was high they had all the flint they could pack. Let us go we can take no more. So they rode south, young boys' rode north, only braves rode south. They rode to old stone breakers lodge and unpacked the white flint with blue lines all came to watch it was the best any one had ever seen. I have looked, all the time, and never found any thing like this. Is there more? There is more, good. Tall Elk put his arm on Skunk's shoulder I see my friend you took boys and came back with braves in just three suns.

Touches The Wind asked stone breaker for some points so Skunk could make arrows to fit his new bow. For now Tall Elk gave him some and a quiver to put them in, now go shot but pick up the arrows. Tall Elk told his son, your mother would like more antelope skins and some mule deer skins. Ask five boys to hunt with you. Take our spirit guides and eagle take pack horses too. Six maybe go when you are ready. I will get the horses. Take Frog, Fat Legs and three more. Moon Boy called the pack and told them they were ready, the she wolf called eagle Skunk said he would like to go. All said Ho so he went. Touches The Wind, He Dog and Worm all wanted to go. Moon Boy said let us go then, so they did.

He pulled the bay around took the lead and pointed west at a fast canter, past the old camp, past the den up over the ridge to cedar draw were he pulled to a stop. Curly, Cubby and Sniff go see if the big buck bounder is here, no but some little bucks are over that hill. We will leave them for now and get antelope. The hunters went up on the flats west by a little north over the next rise prong horns grazed. Moon Boy turned left up over a low ridge, and found low hill to his liking.

He got two long sticks. One he put a white skin on the other a red skin he stuck them in the ground, turned and grinned. Get your bows now we lay down we will see. Antelope has perfect vision; they can see a long way of very well. But if they can't make since out of it, it bothers them. A buck looked up from grazing saw the skins fluttering on the hill. What was it? Now more looked nothing. No movement, just a little flutter. An old buck stomped nothing, some younger bucks pranced forward stopped, the thing just stayed there. The old buck was getting mad.

By now ten or so were clustered around all looking. The old buck could stand it no longer. He would stomp it, bad choice three arrows took him in the air. Five prong horns were down, three more were wounded one not to bad. Skunk shot one way of with his big bow. The two took more arrows and was down. Moon Boy sent the pack to get the other antelope. Touches The Wind had arrows in two antelopes and all helped to get the innards out. The pack had the last one down now.

Moon Boy called them back, so they could eat and eagle to. Skunk said, "Get the arrows you shot." They loaded the antelope got the one the pack killed, Moon Boy got his flags let us take the meat to camp I am hungry. The way back to camp was fast all were in a hurry to eat antelope, it was that good. Tall Elk said Ho. Did they jump on the horses to? All but one we had to help him on. He was laughing to much he though it funny for good smart antelope to stand in line to die, for watching a flag flutter in the wind.

Sweet Grass and Doves Tail skinned the antelope and told Tall Elk, now we have enough skins to make you a dress to, would you like one plain or decorated? Skunk thought this funny he laughed so hard he fell over tears running down his face a chiefs dress ho, ho, ha and more tears fell. Tall Elk said, If this one is tired of rolling around on the ground getting his face dirty, may be we can eat. Tall Elk called a council of all the head braves, and some of the women. What do we have more then we need. We should go trade with the growers on the big waters, far to the east, and north. Get corn seeds, pumpkins and other things they grow. We have many buffalo robes. Taken Alive said we could trade. Skunk said we have bows and I can make more and meat we could kill when we get there. We need bags to bring things back in. We need pack horses may be thirty of them. Do we have that many pack saddles? No, but we can use robes to bundle some things in we will ask the spirit guides to go and one eagle. Two eagles we will leave to watch the camp. Moon Boy asks five boys to go, Skunk ask four helpers to go, and fifteen more braves and I will go. Looking Back Horse you and Iron People be chiefs and take care of the band. We will go when all is ready.

Moon Boy call our spirit guides and eagles. They were there ask the she wolf to have two eagles to watch the camp. We will be gone ten suns, may be. Do some of you want to stay? No, the pack should stay together. Moon Boy asked the she wolf if she would ask eagle to go east and north to the bigger river and see if she could find people growing crops. So they could trade with them, eagle was gone.

Tall Elk came to talk to his son. Father I asked eagle to go look by the river east and north to see if growers are there, good my son you did well. I was going to ask you to do that, now we will wait for her return. Two suns later eagle was back. She ate meat and told Moon Boy her findings. Yes, there are growers along the river on two sides, but this year's crop is little yet. You should go and see if they will trade, then take your robes and things to trade. Tall Elk told what eagle said all said to go. Take only a little of what they had some robes, some bows, some dried meat, old stone breaker had some good knives and points made. We could go and look see what they had take pack horse may be get more flint, on way back. Yellow Footed Dog should go. He knows where to find flint. One Skunk should go he can get better wood for a better bow. Always, we must get better, our lives depend on it. We are the best now but we can get better. Fill your quivers with our best. Get the best bows the strongest lances and start at first light.

When sun was back a long line of horse men were going north by east, at a steady pace. Moon Boy was up front with the pack, Curly to his right and Cubby on the left the she wolf Sniff and Dusty Rose in front Blue Dawn at Curly's right the rest behind the prancing bay. Eagle floated high over head watching. Behind Moon Boy came the five boy braves Frog Fat Legs, Worm, Touches The Wind and He Dog. Tall Elk came with the others nineteen in all, followed by the six pack horses. They past the Grand River and were on the flat lands north east moving at a fast trot, then a canter now a rolling lope back to a walk. Up ahead were lake beds filled by spring rain here they stopped watered the horses and themselves too. They let the horses graze, rest and they ate dried meat.

The country was dotted with buffalo and other game. It was green and lush and went on to the sky line, where soft clouds floated and made shadows on the land. The breeze was warm and sweet. Meadow larks were singing close and far, giving sounds like a fine musician tuning up for a concert. Tall Elk mounted his white stallion, all the rest getting their horses and travel resumed at swinging lope. To the northeast the brakes of the Missouri River could be seen it had been a long sun. Some of the horses were showing signs of getting tired so the riders slowed to a walk. Looking for a camp sight they found a stream with some wood and made camp. Skunk saw ten buffalo grazing near by and killed a young dry cow.

Fires were kindled, the cow skinned, the hide pegged out, scraped and soon hump ribs were cooking along with steaks of the hind quarters. Meat was given, eagle and the spirit guides some liver, all the lung and most of the heart all ate well. The horses were rubbed down with dry grass, watered again and put on grass. One Skunk worked the hide more. Put ashes and brains on it now it was tanned, when sun came it would be rolled and put with the rest. Not much was ever wasted.

Sun was down and twilight had covered the land. More meat was cooked for the ones still hungry and then robes were put by the fires and most slept. Curly, Cubby and Blue Dawn lay down by Moon Boy. The rest acting as night guards they would trade off a wolf would be on guard all night. Sun was coloring the east and the fires were lighted and meat was cooking all got up made water. Then water skins filled, a new sun had come. Horses were packed after the Sioux had eaten, all started out they did not push the horses.

They had a long run and they needed time to warm up. By mid sun they were near the big river it laid in front of them, wide and flat and on a raised bench of ground crops were growing Long rows of plaints of some kind, braves, women, and children were tending the fields. Tall Elk and the Sioux just watched. They could do that maybe. They had river land and water. Up river on this side sat the grower's camp.

Let us go talk, Moon Boy hold our spirit guides in. Tell them to stay in our middle, he did they rode off the hill in to the main camp. Some braves come out Tall Elk raised his right arm palm out, the plain sign for peace. I am Tall Elk chief of this band of Sioux. We come to trade with you. We come far we would talk. I am Blue Corn, here I am chief. You are welcome, Tall Elk. What can you trade? We did not bring a lot. We knew your crops would not be ready yet but we have buffalo robes bows, dried meat, and flint arrow points some, knifes. We could go kill buffalo for you. That is good. I see you have wolves with you. Yes, they are our spirit guides they help us in the hunt in battle and watch my son. He does not see well, he sees with their eyes. Will you eat with us? Yes then we will trade.

The horses were put on grass, given water, all waited for Blue Corn, and then he was there. They brought out large dishes and bowls of steaming food. Corn cakes, stewed squash and pumpkin, corn mush with meat in it, green beans with something more in it, something green with large leaves cooked all was very good how will we cook it? We don't know how, you will learn, we will tell you.

Buffalo were many out on the flats, Skunk take the braves and go kill some buffalo twenty or so get poles of that pile to make drags, we may need the skins to take back, Moon Boy you and the boys help me. Get the pack horses. Tall Elk asked Blue Corn, "What are you going to do with the buffalo". The braves will kill twenty or more, build fires in a row put racks over fires and dry the meat, cook some fresh. Can corn be planted now? And will it grow? It is getting late but it could make corn you will water it if it gets dry. Plant two seeds in ground, this deep he showed him on his finger dig up ground this big around corn. Plant other seeds same way. Show me what you have. Blue Corn made a sign and his people got many things out to see, dry pumpkins and squash, beans, corn seeds pumpkin squash seeds, water melon seeds. Now when other plants grow by your crop you must pull them up by hand, or they take over and no crop. Show me bowls dish, when you cook them dry put them in water and soak them, maybe one sun. Put dry peppers in for taste all so salt from alkali spots. Do you have long knifes? Some let me see. By this time fires were burning with racks, the braves were coming Blue Corn get your people, the meat must be cut thin and hung over fire we will help. Skunk and the others showed how to cut thin and hang over racks. Soon all were cutting, hump ribs and steaks were cooking large pot were brought out water put in, meat cut up and boiling.

The spirit guides had gone with the braves so they ate out where the buffalo were killed. Blue Corn, put some pepper and salt in the boiling meat. Not more then that or you will spoil it. More racks were set up, more fires, and still a lot of meat was left to use. Skunk and his helpers worked on the skins scraped and cleaned them and put brains and ashes on and rubbed it in. Now it must dry.

Sacks of corn, pumpkin, bean, squash, and water melon seeds were put in a pile, Blue Corn said keep seeds dry or they will sprout, then they will not grow. Also keep horses and buffalo out of your crops or they will eat them. Corn and bean seed can be soaked and cooked in your pots. The other seeds are only good for planting, and they grow on vines and were a flower is a vegetable will form. I will send more sacks of bean and corn. You can eat them anytime, but remember soak beans and corn one sun, before cooking. You should grind corn to a powder then make it damp then put it in your oven and bake it. I will show you how to make an oven, I will show Skunk, and his helpers they can do it.

Dried peppers were put in bags, now pumpkins and squash were tied in rolls they were dried and cut in rings. Last long knives were brought out, and three pots for cooking. Also bowls for dishing up were sent and a few ax for digging. The pots had been cooking and simmering all sun. Beans and corn put in at different times, now it was time to sample the food, Tall Elk, Moon Boy and Skunk were given first they had never ate anything so good, now all were fed, and fed again it was that good. The spirit guides and eagle were fed but not out of the pots, they got meat not good for cooking and scraps. All ate well, then were given a pumpkin pudding, all ate again. Some braves inwards was bubbling like the pots had all sun, they slipped of to leave their waste on the hill sides.

Moon Boy got his robe and lay down, as before the pack lay all around him guarding him all night. When sun was back the things traded for was loaded and tied in place. The bows and some of the robes the points some flint knives, were left as well. The dried meat Tall Elk gave as a gift, bring back the sacks when you come back this fall we can use them again. The new robes covered the seeds in case it rained.

All were horse back so they left, up over the hill and on the flat lands at a gentile canter every thing was riding well, so they moved to a swinging lope to cover ground faster when the horses were slick with sweet, they slowed to a walk to let them blow. At mid sun they watered at the stream and let them graze a little, packs was looked at, then they were moving at a long lope. They stopped at the lake beds and watered again, then on at a walk the horses got to much water and were sloshing a bit, so they walked them until they let go some yellow water.

Now the pace was faster again, the canter was a good gate to set, so they rode it. Long shadows pointed behind them. When they got to the brakes of the Grand River Skunk got a lucky long shot and a grand bull elk fell, six points, the Skunk had more horns for knife handles. The elk was skinned, fires were lighted and soon the meat was cooking. Packs were taken of horses so they could roll in the dust. Skunk scarped the hide pegged it out put brains and ashes on it and let it dry. This elk was much larger then the first, so Skunk and others built fires to dry some of the meat so it would not be lost to spoil. It was just too good to lose. It was close to sun down, so some of the braves got their robes and got comfortable by the fires they smoked and talked and remembered the good food just past, all looked forward to planting the seeds so they to could eat the good things out of their fields. If they knew how much work it took to grow crops they may not have been existed. They did not, so they were. By mid sun they were back in camp, and went to work. Tall Elk picked long bench of land by the river. They formed teams some digging and fluffing up the soil, others pulling up grass routs. Some planting seeds they planted pumpkins squash and water melons first. They changed off often so no one person got to tired.

Other teams were planting corn and beans, a row of corn a row of beans as Blue Corn told them. When ten rows of pumpkins, squash, and melons were planted a half mile long. They moved to help the corn and bean planters. When you get the entire band working in teams, with a single goal in mind much can be done in a hurry. When sun fell of the edge of the world, a very tired group came back to camp. The ones who stayed in camp had food cooked all ate and were soon sleeping.

When sun came back Tall Elk called a short council, my brother and sisters, we have planted a crop of food. No one person is to take care of it we all will. One thing we must do is build a lodge to hang our seeds and put our crop in. If they get wet they will not grow. Last sun we planted ten rows of pumpkins, squash and melons and five rows of beans and five rows of corn. Now let plant the rest of the corn some of you build a large lodge, to hang seeds in. The rest who can, lets plant corn.

By mid sun ten more rows of corn was planted. When the planters got back the frame for a large lodge was in place and many braves and women had lodge cover about ready to go up. All ate. Moon Boy ask ten or more boy braves to hunt with you go kill some buffalo and antelope and what ever else you find. We will soak beans and corn maybe some pumpkins and squash. We will set up the cooking pots. When sun comes next we will see. Take drags and our spirit guides Moon Boy and young braves got poles ropes and their bows and rode west past mule deer draw to where antelope were grazing.

Moon Boy put the stick up with skin on top and waited. It is kind of funny you can do some things a hundred times and they work and the next time nothing. Well no prong horns were coming, so the boys rode east found a group of buffalo, killed two bulls and a dry cow they tock out the in sides the pack ate some the boy ate some liver after much pushing and rolling got them on the drags and rode east. Moon Boy asked Curly and Cubby to look in mule draw to see if any deer were there. In a little steep draw some last years young were bedded down bow strings twanged and three young bucks never know what hit them.

The boys got them ready, loaded them, eagle wanted two deer hearts. The spirit guides ate the rest. Moon Boy took them across the draw, and down the boney ridge over to were it forked then up the left side. Going was slow pulling the drags but like anything you do, if you are determined enough you can and will do what must be done. They were at the old camp now going was better and faster. They came around bend of the river and rode in to camp.

Tall Elk came over to the boys and said you have done very well, all of you. I am proud to be your chief. You have done the work of full grown braves. The buffalo are full grown, and very heavy, and yet boys of ten summers have killed them, loaded them and brought them back to us. Come let us skin and cut up the buffalo and deer, you young braves watch and see we do it well, then I will show you the new lodge were the seeds are kept. Sweet Grass and Doves Tail skinned out the deer and hung them up ready for putting them in the new pots. One Skunk took over the job of pegging out the new buffalo skins. Then he and Yellow Footed Dog and The Skunk You Can Not See cut up the meat to go in the pots half full of water. The women did the same with the deer saving back enough for the evening meal. They knew Moon Boy liked it.

The wood and small branches were put near by to start the fires when all was ready. Beans and corn was soaking, wild onions and wild turnips were in piles. Buffalo horn spoons for taking of the impurities. Tall Elk asked Moon Boy and the other boys to come a see the new lodge, known as the seed lodge. They did, it was much larger then other lodges.

The seed sacks hung head high from the ground. A fire was burning to dry out any water or dampness in seed. Skunk and his helpers had started work on the ovens. A raised flat rock floor was done, with heavy wood stakes covered with clay coming up to form a dome. The door way large enough to pass the tray in and out with corn cakes to bake. A hard wood fire would be lighted in the oven. When all was ready the cakes would be baked, but first corn had to be ground. This puzzled Skunk.

He sat in the seed lodge with the boys and Tall Elk. I need round smooth rocks big I all so need a flat rock large. He asked one of the boy braves to go find his helpers, they came. Go to the river were water runs over rocks, find five or six big as you can round rocks, then find a large flat rock bring them. Take horse and drag may be two flat rocks. The braves were gone a long time, when they returned they had the round rocks.

Skunk looked them over carefully. Three were good, two would work. The flat rocks would work with some hollowing out of the center. Skunk asked for Stone Breaker he came. I need the flat rocks hollowed out in the center. The corn goes in the center. Then we roll the round rock over the corn grinding the corn, can you do that? Yes I think I can good do you need help? May be some one could turn the stone as I work on it. That would help "when"? Now, I would like to try grinding the corn. Get a robe so we do not spill any ground corn.

Skunk spread out the robe do any one have a bag? One of the boys thought his mother had one so he got it. Good now we will see. Skunks helpers brought the first of the flat rocks, all hollowed out good we will try. They put it in the middle of the robe, Skunk got some corn and put it in the center, he got a round stone and rolled it back and forth over the corn some of the corn crumbled showing its white insides then more, the more he rolled it the finer it got good now how do we get it in bag? We need to carve a peace of wood thin on one side and long, tapered and smooth, with a little curve to pick up corn to put it in bag. Ask Bears Tale, he is all ways carving, he can do it go ask him we will show him, they did. Yes. I will do it, well.

Now sun was here, a woman was but in charge of a cooking pot under Tall Elk who knew how to cook, from Blue Corn. Fires were lighted under each pot Tall Elk told the women to keep a steady fire at all times. He told them when the meat started boiling a foamy impurities would form on top. This was to be taken off. Tall Elk told them to keep water at a level like now. In a little time all pots were bubbling, and brown foam was forming on top. This they took of. Stir often so it don't stick to pot, the chief nodded and the bean and corn was added to each pot, now cut up the onions and turnips they were added to the mixture Now stir often.

At mid sun I will add the dry peppers and alkali powder then it must bubble until we eat our feast. We have some pumpkins and squash in water. Cut of the out sides and put them in pots. Tall Elk added the dry peppers and alkali powder now it is finished now we shall see add water so it keeps full to here. Tall Elk said, four boy braves get horse and bows and quivers, two on each side of the crops. Keep buffalo and horse out of crop. Trade of so no one guards stays to long.

Along about sun down the feast began, all was merriment, talking, laughing, and eating. A lot of back slapping hand shaking, the words most spoken was I never ate anything so good in my life before. And of course not, anyone ever had the chance to eat much more then meat because that's all there was. With the exception of wild turnips, wild onions rose tips, berries, and some green. No vegetable that was new and tasted wonderful. They simply ate it all to the last drop, so to speak. That was good; no one could have eaten more any way.

Wind came from the south east; it had a soft warm moist feel about it. Way off in the west you could hear thunder rolling. Low at first, then more flashes could be seen, the rains were coming. Good, the soil would be set on the crops and watered. More rumbling, more flashes, the wind stopped, calm rains felt like light rain. More and more rains came. Soon a heavy rain was falling sounding like drums on the lodge covers. Dark it was very dark, the rain still fell, but less now. More like a soft pitter pat sound then a soft breeze that smelled like moist earth, mixed with flowers came floating in the lodges.

The Sioux people were full, warm and sleepy, so they slept. When sun brought light back to the world it was a clean world, fresh and washed. Like a baby face, the breeze was cool and sweet and the sun would soon be shinning. Good growing sun for the crops. Soon they would be up, and then the real work would begin. Tall Elk and some braves washed out the cooking pots and then put them away, in the seed lodge.

When sun came out the women and girls pulled ropes tight to hang out sleeping robes to air and dry. Always some water got under the lodge covers to get things wet; no one seemed to mind too much. The pack came by and ate some meat. Moon Boy explained to them, Curly and Cubby, the crops will be growing soon we will be guarding them from the horse and buffalo so they don't eat them or step on them. You could run down the though the rows and keep out the rabbits eat all you want keep horse out to. Moon Boy asked, "Have you seen eagle"? No not for two suns is all well with her? Yes I think so mother asked her to fly west and south. Mother thinks some one is coming again. You are rich you have many horse and much to take. They think you grow careless, they don't think we, your spirit guides or eagles are with you any more.

Some of us run one way the rest of us run the other every night. A tight circle around camp, we have found nothing yet but be ready I will get father. Moon Boy got Tall Elk and sat down with Curly and Cubby and told the chief all. Ho this is not good news, I thought they would rather live then die. Call Skunk, he came and Curly told him all. Skunks ask your helpers and Moon Boy with six brave boys to help. Take five more good braves, take Looking Eagle get wood for many strong bows. Get flint take pack horses, I will get good braves to go kill some buffalo. When you get back, we will eat well again. Tall Elk asked boys to guard the crops. Go as soon as you can.

Chapter Ten

One Skunk got ready and soon was riding north toward the Grand River seven braves and seven brave boys. The spirit guides and eagle, two eagles stayed to fly over the land watching. Tall Elk asked the arrow makers to make more arrows, just a little longer then the rest. The going was fast Skunk and his braves made good time. They were at the Grand River about mid sun, Skunk asked Yellow Footed Dog to take six with him and get flint out of the place of flint. Skunk took the others to the hill sides, were oak and ash and cider grew. He liked standing dead wood better, but he was taking some wood not full seasoned, it would work just as well maybe. Just before middle sun Skunk had wood for may be thirty or more new bows, ash, oak and cider. Yellow Footed Dog had gotten some good flint loaded on the pack horses all starter back to camp.

The news of more pending trouble was not good news, no one wanted more war with anyone, in war you had to kill, and some times it was you that got killed and that did not set well, with your evening meal. The back trail was slower; the horses were not fresh but did rest some while the braves worked. They moved at a canter then a long lope, and then back at a trout they walked to let the horses blow. They found a stream and watered the horses not to much, just enough to keep them going. In a grassy draw, they let the horses graze when most of the horses had left piles of used grass they rode again.

The Moreau River breaks were in sight now, as they rode in to the first of the breaks. The shadows were long pointing east, and then they were in camp they unloaded the flint at stone breakers lodge the bow wood at Skunks lodge, rubbed down the horses and put them on grass. All were tired and hungry and glad to be back in camp. Tall Elk came and said Ho, and my brothers you are fast I am glad to see you, now come and eat so they did. One of the pots had been bubbling. All sun long soon it was disappearing down bellies of the braves and it was good. Curly and Cubby and the pack ate. It was time to go look out in the dark.

They had no equal they saw you heard you or smelled you, near or far it made no difference and then their animal instincts took over. They knew you were out there. If you were enemies of the band, and meant harm they knew and you had problems, no better group of scouts was ever formed, and when the pages of this book are closed, are likely never to be again. Curly found a lone horse track going in a straight line. He thought it better be looked in to so he called the pack, they followed along and found the rider, he was looking at the camp and never saw them. When he did he jumped for his horse. No good they were all around him. He tried to run that was funny three had him down in two jumps. Now Cubby looked in his face and let his terrible sound slide out over his gleaming fangs. The brave was not of the band, so was an enemies.

He was pushed and prodded to camp the pack took him to Tall Elks lodge Curly got the chief and son up, Curly told Moon Boy see what we found looking at the camp? Just then the scout's horse was brought to camp by the pack. the brave's eyes were as big as cow pies. Tall Elk signed who are you and what are you called? I am known as Tree Frog I am a Pawnee what do you want with us? I am looking for Tall Elks band of Sioux and when you find them? We will take their horse heard and any thing we want, they are week now with their wolves gone Tall Elk hit him in the mouth, and who brought you to camp? And your horse to, I think you are stupid our spirit guides brought you in son of a snake.

I am Tall Elk. By now other braves were standing near take his knife and bow, let me see them. Moon Boy took the knife I will cut worms with this, he took the bow for my sister, she is little but she can play with it all this with sign talk. The Pawnee turned color first red then a sickly white, he had heard of what happened to Bent Feather the crow, and thought he was next. We thought they were no longer with you, and eagle to? No we have three eagles now and one more wolf. It is cool, take of every thing even foot ware. You will stand by post until we give you to the wolves, when you come to kill and steal we will kill you and steal your life. You have a good horse. I will give it to my son. You will ride no more.

The Pawnee signed, before you tie me, hear my words let me go, and we will go back not to bother you again. You should not have come at all. The pack will find your war party now then we will see. Tie him to the post put water on him it may warm him. Curly and Cubby go find them see how many they are, some stay others come and tell us, we will wait.

The pack found them eight miles south camped in a wooded draw. All were asleep in their robes. Tall Elk with twenty braves grabbed up the ten braves tied them hand and foot and took them back to camp. When they got back Tall Elk thanked their spirit guides for once again saving some band members life. Had they not found the one scout the sun would have came up short. Horses and lives to they jerked the captives of the horses, made sure they were tied and asked the pack to watch until light came.

At first light Tall Elk asked who is chief a small brave said I am, so his hands were untied so he could sign talk. Do you see the one tied by the post? Our spirit guides found him making water and caught him by themselves, and caught you too and could have killed you all and maybe will. But I Tall Elk would ask you why you are here? You had better speak with straight tongue or the wolves will kill you one at a time and we will watch. Now talk, what is your name? I am Wood Duck; we came to take your horses and kill you and take what you have. And now? We will die, we were told the wolves left and you were care less, Tall Elk got his hair and pulled him out in the middle take off all no I will not the ax hit with a thump. Tall Elk took his hair. Untie them, not the one at the post now take off all they did. You came to take ours now we got yours; brave boys pick a horse, Fat Lag, pick one, Frog and the rest of you pick one. Untie him, take off all, we knew you were coming a long time. Get the horses. They were there to pick him up and go back to your country; we will see you do now run.

Raw hide ropes snapped on bear skin. Cubby made his sounds and the race was on for ten miles they run now rest Tall Elk said, put him on the ground, cover him with rocks go kill one buffalo, it was done. Tall Elk dropped two knives on the ground, now go build a fire. The ten Pawnee got wood branches and old bird nest from near by, some soap weed stems for fire sticks. Soon a little smoke was curling up then tiny tongues of flame ate at the bird nest then they had fire. Skin that buffalo and get some meat cooking. If it was me, I would make foot ware out of that skin you have a long way to walk.

Tall Elk helped soon all were helping. They made more fires for cooking Tall Elk cut a hump rib and cooked it, so did others. There was enough skin to make crude foot ware with some left for lacing.

Now hear me, your chief who lies under the rocks. Wood Duck told me, he came to kill us and take our horses and anything we had he wanted. Where is he now? Look under the rocks you can find. I Tall Elk say to you, you are lucky all of you should be with your chief, under the rocks but we the Sioux people are good. We don't kill for the fun of it but when we do kill we do it well, I don't know your names but I know your faces and I say this if you. Come again to do us harm you will be under the rocks with Wood Duck. I Tall Elk have spoken! Remember we have eight wolves helping us scout three eagles overhead they see all, and my son can talk to them and they to him. No one can take us by surprise, now go and live.

They cut meat, put out the fires and went south. Clumsy in their new foot wear, but go they did at a fast pace. Tall Elk and the braves watched them go, then turned and went back to camp. The pack fanned out looking for signs. Eagle over head was watching far and close. An unbeatable team any enemies should know not to try to get through, but always some would. The crops were up, tiny green plants showing in each dug up circle round flat leaves were pumpkins, squash and water melon. Tall thin plants with long leaves were corn, smaller round leaves were beans.

Ho! Tall Elk said we will celebrate. Come some of you go get fresh meat, others get wood. We will need water to cook with and onions and wild turnips for taste. Hurry now we will eat when sun falls off the world in the far west. Tall Elk dismounted at One Skunks lodge. Ho, my friend I would set with you and smoke with you. Maybe, you are welcome Tall Elk, they lighted the pipe. The crop is up we will celebrate I sent braves to get the things we need, we will eat when sun is low.

How are the bows coming are they are very strong? I like the oak bows; do you need a new one? No I am just now getting to understand this one, it is a good one. Did you look at the Pawnee bows? Yes they are shorter then ours and not as powerful as ours. Do you see anything about them we could improve on? No they are just bows, and the arrows. They are shorter, but would kill just not as far away as ours put them to one side we will trade them to the growers this fall for food. What did you think of their horses? Most of them were common, not good, not bad just horses. One or two maybe could run fast I have not tried them. You gave them to our brave boys, and they are fine for them.

The crow horses are much better. The Pawnee have nothing we want I think. I was thinking have you seen any thing in the wild horses we want? I have heard of a cream colored stallion with white main and tail who ranges far west, past the crow lands on the slopes of the big mountains, called the Rockies. He may not be there now, he may be dead or some one else has him. We must be sure before we go fifteen suns one way, only to find him gone, of course Skunk you are right we will ask the others. Come let us see how the pots are bubbling the crops were up and that was important.

The big stallion would be free until someone captured him. They put in the onions wild turnips and dry peppers alkali powder and now the corn and beans so they could cook longer, all was ready. Tall Elk cleared his wind pipes the crops are up. A shout went up now all of us must watch. Now we must keep out buffalo, horses and deer even at night. We must form a crop guard of boys, braves and women change often so no one stays to long. We should all take our turn even me. When we guard, ride horse take your good bow and quiver, kill rabbits good to eat and they eat crops for guards at a time. If you can not go, get someone to go for you. In three suns we will all go to take out any plaints we don't need. Be careful as not to take out a good plant.

Moon Boy ask the pack to come in, they were. Curly when you see eagle ask her to talk to Moon Boy. As by magic three dots became three eagles gliding in to sit by Moon Boy he had food for them they ate.

Eagles far to the west past the land of the crow and over near the tall mountains ranges. A golden stallion with silky white main and tail we would like to know, if he is free or is he dead or is he captured, and does he have suns we could catch or is he guarded by some tribe. This we would like to know. Eagle looked wise. I have seen the one you ask about not long past. He is not well. He was beaten and is no longer king. One of his grandsons is now king and is not golden. The new king is more bronze with silver main and tail but is mean and has killed braves who wanted him. I will ask him if the old king feels like coming and with that she was gone. Moon Boy told his father all. Tall Elk was disappointed. He would have liked to catch him or some of his sons but wild things had a short season of life. They spent too much energy just living, it was true then, it is true now.

It was long shadow time the pots had been bubbling for most of a sun, and the steam was good to smell, every one was hungry. It was about time to eat so they did. They took a long time at it enjoying every bite. Skunk got up and got some golden corn cake and gave some to Tall Elk. I am not sure if this is the way to do this or not, but it is good we should get some honey and try that; yes I think honey would be good.

Two suns had gone by; when sun came they all would be in the fields taking out plaints called weeds. Light was back, the entire band except the old and young or the people who were cooking were ready to start. Skunk, Looking Back Horse, Yellow Footed Dog and Looking Eagle had been shown by Blue Corn the grower chief how to proceed, the for got down and with their knifes and first showed the people what a pumpkin was corn and the other crop so no one would take out a food plant and leave a weed. They took the knife point and took out anything not a crop. When this was done they loosened the soil in the rest of the circle making the soil dark in color. See, that is how it is done and moved to the next circle soon every row of crop was being tended, workers moved a long way down field, and started again. Then the workers from behind would catch up and move past, go down field and start again, the entire time changing of so some could rest most of the time.

Tall Elk was a hard worker, making his circle bigger then he found it as did many of the others. Sweet Grass and Doves Tall worked side by side chatting about the new baby coming and about just nothing or anything. They sat down and other workers took their place. Tall Elk looked back and was surprised, they had tilled way over half the crop, and only half way to mid point it was wonderful to see the new green plants against dark soil. The crop guards sat their horses with bow ready.

The pack watched far and near, Tall Elk white stallion stood near by with his bow and quiver hung on him small boys tending them. He got on the stallion and roe slowly to were a circle had a large amount of weeds and grass growing with the crop The Skunk You Can Not See was cleaning it, Ho my brother that is full of weeds. Not now he grinned I have made it look like soil again, you should rest. I will soon my back says it is tired. Moon Boy and some boy braves worked together, they were proud of their work. Ho said Tall Elk we will eat well this snow time, you are doing good thank you my chief.

Tired workers came out to sit and rested workers took their places. A little past sun's mid point the crop was tended, the workers splashed in the river, and went to camp food was ready so they ate. Tall Elk rested then walked to Skunks lodge Skunk and his helpers were shaping bows and gluing horn strips on, for more power some were lasted with wet raw hide by the middle for a better hand hold.

One Skunk said I was thinking, we need tools for working the soil, I will talk with stone breaker. I have a plain. Skunk and Tall Elk with Looking Back Horse walked to old Stone Breakers lodge. Skunk asked, "How goes it with you, my brother"? I am well. Skunk said, "I am thinking we need some tools for working the soil. Maybe a tool like a knife only lying down and straight with the cutting edge under it so, it would cut the weeds off, just under the top of the soil. It should be about as long as tall braves first finger, or maybe just a little more. How will it be fixed to the stick? Skunk said you make one. I will fix it. I think, we will see, it should not be wide or too heavy. Stone Breaker said I like the flint you brought me. It is the best I ever had to work with I will make the tools, when you go back get more, then I will have plenty. Eagle was there, Moon Boy came out and eagle saw him and was there.

I Eagle have news, the golden stallion is coming Tall Elk came and sat down , he has some of his wives with him and colts, but the crows want him to stay he only moves at night. He wants the spirit guides you Moon Boy and some braves to come help him. He has a big stud colt with him he says it is for you, and to be your war horse Moon Boy told his father all. How many braves will you take? I will ask ten brave boys to come and any others you ask. Tall Elk cleared his wind pipes; Eagle has told us the golden stallion is coming. He needs help the crows don't want him to come. Eagle told him all. He wants Moon Boy and the pack to come my son will ask his brave boys, and I will ask you Skunk, Looking Back Horse, Looking Eagle, Runs Fast, Bulls Tail, Spotted Owl, Yellow Footed Dog, The Skunk You Can Not See, Stands Tall and Buffalo Tongue to go with him and more if you want to. Moon Boy said, "We go as soon as you are ready." He asked the pack to come with him and they were ready. The bay stood waiting; Moon Boy filled his quiver, got his bow, his knife his robe and was ready. Tall Elk put two eagle feathers in his hair and put a white line under each eye, hear Skunk he is wise.

Eagle led the way Moon Boy spoke to the bay he was of like an arrow away from the bow. Moon Boy held him in he wanted to run so he danced sideways then line out again the others formed a double line fowling two by two, before one could say pull that weed they were out of sight and gone.

Thunder was rolling out from under the horses hooves. Moon Boy felt like a king. He in fact was a king, boys did not normally lead war parties and no one would have followed. But here they were dashing along behind a boy chief's son. Trying not to get in fight with the crows that had about all they could from a certain band of Sioux. You may say their noses had been rubbed in it once to often. All the horses were running nicely now. That first burst of speed was past they were warmed up and running smoothly. The ground slid away as if by magic.

Curly on the right Cubby on the left Blue Dawn, Sniff and mother in front, the rest fanned out in back. Eagle overhead was leading the way. Moon Boy pulled the bay to a walk to let them blow on the next hill they stopped. Eagle sat down and said they are coming now. The stallion was moving slowly, he had came a long way and was tired and hurt as well, are there anyone following? Not close but yes how many two here one over there five back all looking. We should go and get there first a short run if we hurry, so they did.

The moon was shinning on his golden coat coming across the flats. The Sioux got down letting the stallion take his troop through. The crow was pounding along thinking they were getting more horses; the Sioux mounted in a long line. The pack came up out of the grass the long bows twanged two or three crows were knocked off their horses one more slumped over. Stand yelled Bulls Tail in crow. The other three unhurt braves did. Hands up or more arrows will fly, they did, come here and set. The downed braves, two would not worry about horses again the other three may if cared for. Moon Boy asked the pack to watch them and one of them was Bird Wing, Cubby come and say something to your friend. Cubby walked up and made his sound, and the brave past out... Coward! They pulled the arrows one brave was hit in the belly, he would not see sun, and their horses were spent.

After resting they could go you take this horse and put him on it. Moon Boy said we take your horses and your war things, put rocks on two and maybe this one. Then you can walk back to your camp. It is a long way good, you should have stayed there, and this one should bring more loin clothe so when he soils one, he has more. You Moon Boy said looking at the crow stay here. If you come after us the spirit guides will kill you, or we will. Curly you and the pack watch them. Water is back over that hill we will make camp, while they sleep, come to camp. All the horses were tired so they watered at a spring and let them rest and graze. At first light the pack was in camp. Curly told Moon Boy the crow had left in the night, leaving three on the ground, did they cover them? No then they must stay as they are. The golden stallion and his were not afraid of the wolves or the Sioux, eagle had explained all.

Skunk looked at the stallions wounds, they were many. He washed and cleaned the ones he could, the others were too old to do anything with and were healing on their own. He was stiff and sore swelled up and bit, but his spirit was good, the old king had brought ten older mares with him and six colts, golden like himself with differences, some lighter others darker mane and tail too varied in color. One was perfect he was beautiful in every way, he had the light golden color of the king with white main and tail, white for legs and a white star set between his wide set intelligent eyes. He was deep in the chest and long of leg a short back that connected to powerful hind quarters, and when he moved he took the jar in his fetlocks. Letting him seem to float over the ground like silk over a marble stare way. The braves with Moon Boy looked and looked at the grand colt, and somehow you got the feeling that they were all about to cheer and salute.

Two braves had killed a young buffalo, brought it in the fires were lighted and soon meat was cooking the pack and eagle ate first, they liked theirs uncooked so all were pleased. Skunk put buffalo grease on some of the cuts to keep fly of, others he packed mud on it would dry and fall of but it helped. Some meat was taken tied up in the skin, the rest left to be eaten by anything that came along; they put out the fires and rode east.

The stallion moved better this sun he seemed to feel better with his hurts fixed, he still drug one hind quarter some, but it did not seem to be as bad. Skunk put his hand on Moon Boys shoulder and smiled. If you and our chief don't quit taking horses from the crow they will all be walking, like grandmothers and we will have to hunt for them too, all smiled. Curly put his tongue in the corner of his mouth and winked at Cubby, hunt food for the crow? That was good, but you knew Skunk he was funny even when did not mean to be. The pack all snickered, even Eagle gave a high five all felt good, humor all ways was better then gloom and made going brighter and easer.

Of the seven horses taken from the crow, five were good stallions, gilded when young Moon Boy could take any he wanted but his eyes only saw the golden stud colt. One of the last two was a clay bank mare, with black legs up to her knees, black main and tail. Alert quick head ears trimmed in black, wide flared nostrils a white line that started up above her eyes coming down to her nose. She was a line back a thin black line started at her main and went back to her tail. She looked to be about five years old, high stepping and smooth gated. She showed speed and power.

Moon Boy picked her and the golden stud colt as his, no one was surprised. The last was just a horse, a gilded stud brown in color he would be good for riding crop guard or pulling fire wood or drag poles that would be all. The stallion was moving well now staying behind his group nipping at a mare now and again if she slowed to much, the braves behind and to either side Moon Boy in front, the wolves in their places. That is how they came to the Sioux camp.

Tall Elk was standing grinning from ear to ear Ho my sun and his braves has done very well, I see the golden stallion is with us now, just look at him, he will give us fine colts. Moon Boy proudly rode up to his father, and said some crow wanted him we left three on the ground and for walked back to their camp. I take the clay bank mare and the golden stud colt as mine, the other six the brave boys can pick from all the rest belong to us all, and a grate shout went up. Of the six colts for were studs, Looking Back Horse and Iron People were looking at the plainer darker little studs, we would train them my chief and help Moon Boy with his, good he is a good sun, but is growing to fast for his leggings. The spirit guides have made him a brave before his years. I will slow him down, remember he makes good choices for one so young, Ho they said you must be wise.

It had clouded over about just past mid point and a steady rain was falling in to the night thunder sounded far and near it was a wet night but that was good it was needed the crops were growing fast. Moon Boy, Fat Legs, Frog, and Touches The Wind got their bows and quivers caught their horses and rode to the crop land. Moon Boy had the clay bank mare he just tock from the crows. It was still wet, but the sun was shining, making each drop of water like rain bows on the plaints. The vine plants were starting to run. Corn was six inches tall, and the different shades of green stood out on the dark soil the pack were along never to far from Moon Boy at any time.

They ran down the rows chasing out rabbets that liked bean leaves, when they were out of the field the pack ate them. The horse heard was on the other side of the Moreau River watched by the horse guard, just now being replaced by others. Eagle sat on a cotton wood tree eating a rabbit Curly had caught for her. The mare had a nice gate and wanted to run, but not now they just sat and enjoyed the cool early sun. Frog looked all around and drew in a full breath of air. The crops do well we should eat good when snows come again, you are right Fat Legs said. Moon Boy was looking far south. I see some thing I think. Touches the Wind looked and saw many buffalo coming give the signal they must be turned we can not stop them there are to many. The signal was given braves come on horse bows and lances and fire.

Chapter Eleven

Get torches the heard was coming to fast the braves rode to turn them the pack stayed with Moon Boy. He lost his hold and the mare bolted in to the leading edge of the buffalo. He killed a cow then one more Fatty got a bull by the nose and hung on the bull turned in to the heard but they turned more braves came they had them milling more buffalo were killed the unlucky mare stepped in a hole and went down hard, throwing Moon Boy.

The pack kept back the main heard and got them going the other way and it was over. The mare was down two front legs broken. Moon Boy lay still were he was thrown. Fatty was hurt but would live the rest of the pack were fine. All knew the wolves had saved the crop and Moon Boy to if he lived. Tall Elk, Skunk and Looking Back Horse were lifting the boy making him straight. Skunk killed the mare and got the boys things. They took him to camp washed the blood of his head. He lives but that's all said Tall Elk. Go take the meat of the buffalo; we will do what we can for Moon Boy.

They cleaned up Fatty he had broken ribs and some cuts, but he was young and strong. The pack stayed near you could not drive them away, no one tried Skunk could not find bones broke for three suns Moon Boy slept, on the forth sun he asked for water. Then soup was given him, Curly and Cubby lay by him licking his eyes, my head hurts he said. Skunk gave him ground willow bark and water. Sweet Grass fed him soup on the fifth sun he sat up.

The world is going around and around but I can see. I would go out now, they helped him out to sit on a robe, and Skunk came to sit with him. The mare!? No she broke her front legs, she is dead. Moon Boy said, "She bolted and run in the buffalo, I could not hold her." "I know Skunk said. "But why?" Skunk shook his head, she went crazy I think, we can not know. Fatty turned the buffalo and the pack kept them away from you, the pack saved our crops and you. Tall Elk sat down. My son how do you feel? I don't know week hungry and I would drink the river dry, I think. He got water and food the braves came by and he was stronger, I love my wolves, they saved me again. Eagles was there, we saw it from way up, the buffalos were pushed at you by a bad crow, the one you let live, Birds Wing, he is a coward he started them then turned and run. Who was with him? No one he could not get any one to help him, I think they will bring him to you, they have had war with the Sioux and want no more, and they don't want him.

Tall Elk slowly got up I will kill him, no and Cubby growled his terrible sound, he all most killed our Moon Boy, we will kill him it will be slow, but we will do it, all growled yes we will do it. Moon Boy told them what was said. Just what eagle said they are coming! Let Moon Boy take his hair. My bow is it here? Skunk got up. I made a better one for you; the buffalo got your old one, and arrows to. I put your points on new shafts here is your bow and quiver but get stronger first, and then we will eat elk on the Grand River.

Tall Elk came from the fields as many as can, let us go tend crops new weeds have grown and will soon be hurting our food plants. Moon Boy here is your bay just ride and look take your bow and quiver get to know them. Moon Boy mounted and saw how crops had grown in six suns and how many weeds had sprouted in six suns. It was time to till again. A worker was in every row, with new workers to take over when tired workers rested.

Moon Boy rode and looked the vines was spreading out in the grass but that was fine as long as no weeds were by the routes getting water. As all ways Curly and Cubby was with him and Fatty who felt he had saved Moon Boys life by turning the bull and maybe did.

The other pack members laid or just looked on never getting tired of being near him, but look they did they saw all. The she wolf was the first to see the crows coming, still far away and gave the signal; ten crow braves under the white flag were bringing the eleventh Bird Wing with down cast eyes. Moon Boy and ten well armed Sioux and the pack meet them in camp. We are sorry one of us made you trouble, two times he came and you sent him back, now you can have him and his horses we go now in peace. Moon Boy looked long at Bird Wing. Tie him to the post Curly watch him tie the horses too. With that he rode back to the crops.

Moon Boy had taken a good thump on his head, and was dizzy if he turned quick but that to was passing, a few places was still sore when you hit hard like that you must expect to have some pain. But he saw better, a little farther and clearer so that was good.

The workers were about finished tilling the crop it always good to see a job well done, and so far the growing season had been good. Just as the right rain at the right time. Tall Elk was done with the row he was working on, Bird Wing is tied at the post, the crow brought him, and some horses the pack is watching I would like to kill him but our spirit guides want him he will be just as gone, and we would be lost with out them, so do it when you want too, but do it soon. All went to camp.

Moon Boy asked Skunk, the young braves, Iron People, Looking Eagle and Looking Back Horse to come to kill the bad crow. He told the pack, it was time. They rode up to the bad one, you come as a boy we gave you your life back, you came again we did the same. Now you came again to kill and take our food but you are a coward and most killed me. It is your fault, you can never come again. The spirit guides will kill you now out were I was almost killed. Put a rope around his neck tie his hands, we go. Bird Wing was breathing hard no he shouted not the wolves I fear wolves they lead him past the crops see what you all most killed? For what, and down by the dead horse is where I was hurt. You will be here over there is the place Fatty all most died, and you ran away coward. You are not fit to be a crow; you should have been a worm so any one could step on you. When it is done I will take your hair so I can spit on it, your name will not be heard again. Take the rope of, now he is yours the pack circled him he soiled himself again. Fatty cut him Cubby growled, cut him the she wolf broke his arm then freed him. Ling Lang slashed his legs Sniff tore out his in sides. Dusty Rose tore out his seeds and Moon Boy took his hair. Skunk took the hair I will fix it for you, you could put it on your bow no it would be bad luck, and there is no honor in it.

Looking Eagle what would you do with it? I would through it away or put it in the ground, maybe burn it Fat Legs what would you do with it, put it on a stick in the field to chase birds away good that's what we will do go get a long stick. They did it. All felt better. Now let us look at the horses so they did.

Five horses stood waiting, a blue roan mare, sorrel gilding, a pinto mare, a cream and white gilding and a tall black gilding with a white star and one white for leg I will take the sorrel gilding Moon Boy said you take the rest. Eagles came in to camp and talked with the pack Curly came and talked to Moon Boy eagles would eat, so they were given food after eagles ate. They told him some Sioux were on the way five lodges with eight braves and their family. I think they would live with you maybe; you are safe to be near. Hump is with them he is very brave and wise but old now, but still hunts and is no burden. You Tall Elk are well known as a fair chief and they know of the spirit guides and me. They have heard of Moon Boy the boy chief, and of his band of young braves how does grown braves deeds. They are hearing only good things, soon you will be famous, and you grow crops to.

We have heard of a new crop potatoes, very good to eat. They grow in the ground you dig them like turnips you can plant your old field but you should find more, near the one you now have. We will help, from the way up I can tell were crops grow best. It was a long talk for Eagle, but he could if he had something to say, Skunk came to sit. Look at this a flint tool for taking out weeds Tall Elk said does it work? Yes I have tried it, he is making more he would like more flint, are you ready for elk? Yes I am, we will take thirty braves and that many pack horses, I need more bow wood and more flint. Yellow Footed Dog is going get your braves be ready at light. Tall Elk said we will kill some buffalo. We need robes to trade with the growers.

At light, a long line of horses and braves rode north. Skunk was up front, on his black and white pinto stallion just behind him and to his right rode Moon Boy on the bay with white fore legs. Curly on his right and Cubby on his left, three wolves in front and the other three spread out behind, eagle over head there usual marching order. Skunk said to Moon Boy we will get the bow wood and flint first, you take your braves and get wild turnips and onion. Fill the bags if you can they are hard to find on the Moreau. Moon Boy said, Ho and let his bay out a notch the horse gained speed and Skunk let the stallion out just to keep up, in turn kicking up the speed of the column just what Moon Boy wanted, he smiled to himself he was in control and only he knew it. Curly knew and looked over his shoulder and grinned at his boss, who ever said animals were dumb, not me I know better.

They rode five miles at the fast pace before Skunk figured out what Moon Boy did. He looked over and grinned. You will be chief before even I thought I think. The ground slid away under the pounding two hundred and forty hooves as by magic. The thunder of the moving horses over damp sod got the notice of some buffalo grazing, which put their tail in the air and lumbered away making more thunder. Moon Boy tipped his head back and laughed with the joy of living, the air was sweet the grass was green and waved in the breeze from right to left, for as far as you can see and then more. Skunk pulled his stud to a canter then to a walk. Let them blow.

The little stream was there so they watered their mounts not too much. They were hot an needed cooling before letting them have their fill so they grazed back from the water a little. Then mounted rode over to the other side, they were back in motion again, moving in line and covering ground quickly, the brakes of the Grand were now in sight. Soon they would be there and then they were. Yellow Footed Dog and twenty braves with fifteen pack horses broke off the main group and went to get flint. The rest went with Skunk for bow wood. On the far side of the Grand River on the North Slope were trees.

Skunk looked there. Stands of excellent timber for making bows were every place you looked. He was excited. He cut ash, then oak and cedar, then he found more and better so he cut that to. What he cut first he could not leave, so it got on the pile to. Skunk loved his job. He looked at the hillside shook his head, bundle up the bows or I will take them all. As Skunk was about to come out of the red cedars he saw five young bull elk grazing below.

All make ready he signed I want them all. Ten bow strings twanged and four elk fell, one was hit bad but staggered off again the bows bent and the last went down. Good now we eat elk. Bring the bow wood. All worked to skin and clean the meat. The pack ate what Skunk did not want. By the river they made fires and cooked the livers and hearts. Eagle got one of the raw hearts. Skunk put the skins over the meat and tied it in place. They crossed the river and saw the others coming loaded with flint. Go kill a buffalo. Then we will eat, a bunch of twelve buffalo grazed not a hundred feet away. Skunk killed a young bull. Now go build fires I will skin him out they all helped. When the rest got there meat was cooking.

Ho Skunk I see you have wood to arm the camp again, or do you look for wood for cooking. I think you have enough for both. Skunk just smiled. Yellow Footed Dog, did you find flint? Yes better then before and more of it. We could make flint lodges if you said to. The pack looked at each other and smiled. Flint lodges? The man things are crazier then we thought, how would they hear the wind blow, or see the sun? Then it would fall on them, and we would have to dig them out, more work for pack. Curly yawned, stretched and got more comfortable. I am doing all the work now I can stand. Cubby covered his eyes with his paws, Curly and if you get any lazier I will have to bring the kill to you. They loaded the buffalo that was left and started back for camp. Skunk said, "I would like the elk in the cooking pots", so let's go they did. Tall Elk was by his lodge, as they came in Ho you made good time Skunk. I am hungry for elk in the cooking pots. We found wild turnips and onions too so get them set up. I will cut the meat.

Boys were sent for water, fires lighted, elk cut, sliced and set to cook. Each pot had a tender, the corn and beans had soaked long enough and would be put in as soon the meats impurities were off. Wild turnips and onions were in now. The corn and beans had been in for some time, and so had the peppers and salt, with the pumpkin and squash. More water was needed so they put some in. The shadows were long to the east the extra elk was drying in the late sun.

A soft sweet breeze was coming from this way. Life was good on the high plains. As my words are set in type I wonder which world I would have chosen had I the choice. Food is cooked, was the call.

Skunk was the first one to fill his bowl and as it turned out he was the last to put his bowl down. You could say Skunk enjoyed every bite. Moon Boy and three others rode to the crops to guard. They had a surprise waiting for them. Big golden flowers were everywhere. The pumpkins and squash were in bloom the full half mile. Row after row of flowers it was something.

Go get the band they must see. Every one looked amazed at the sight, and Blue Corn the grower chief said for every flower a vegetable would sit and they would set new flowers for suns to come.

The crop was wonderful to look at clean, weed free rows, green plants and now the golden blooms. Proof of what can be done if every one works as one. Tall Elk said maybe we should trade for something, what new bows? Our bow maker just can't keep up with the demand but he is good. His bows put arrows in buffalos far away and have kept the crow looking to make peace, and his wife happy. Come Skunk let us go look at the golden stallion.

Moon Boy ask the pack and eagle to, they found the stallion off by him self. Eagle talked to him is your hurts better? Can you run again? Yes I think I can? Skunk would like to look at you. I like Skunk, he can look. He got off his horse and felt over the big horse, could I sit on your back then you run fast so I can see how you move? Once big cat tried that I bucked him down and killed him but you I will do as you ask. Good Skunk said. Eagle said I will fly near to tell you what Skunk says. Skunk got on the big horse just move around so I can see how you move. He did go faster he did, now run fast over to that hill and back he flew Skunk had never been on a horse like that before.

The wind tore at his hair, his face and he found he was holding on to his mane to stay on. Never had he rode so fast. The golden colt came over to Moon Boy; he was big but trim, with speed written all over him. He patted him rubbed him and made friends with him. Tall Elk the chief would like to ride to, the stallion said yes it felt good to run, so Tall Elk got up the stallion, danced some then broke in to a canter. He felt the chief knee on his right side and turned left, good he pushed the left he went right now Tall Elk said go fast and he did. He felt the wind in his hair his face and the ground was a blur. Tall Elk pushed with his right knee the stallion come left, now back.

They came the chief was having a hard time breathing never had he rode so fast, as they went by Skunk. The stallion turned and came to a stiff legged stop. Tall Elk was glad to be on the ground again, he needed to get his head back on. He was dazed, confused and a little frightened he thought he knew about fast horses but nothing prepared him for this. Skunk shook his head. We have no horse in the heard that could come to his dust. Never have I seen a horse before to equal his speed, we would never have caught him. Tall Elk looked at Skunk. No wonder the crow wanted him so bad he is the reason for their good horses. Next spring we must put our very best mares with him, and then we will see. Skunk said now they will hear of this and try to steel him. No one can steel him the chief said, if he wants to stay with us. We have four of his sons. Moon Boy's and the three lesser ones to work with we will do it, and our own to. Let us go to camp.

Skunk, take ten or more good braves and build a very large lodge. Put up many poles to hang sack's from. We must keep the crop dry and ask women to make bags. Have them put little holes in so air can pass though. Skunk and his helpers started work on the lodge made to store crop.

Tall Elk saw it would take one hundred big bull buffalo to cover the large lodge. I Tall Elk will get hunters, and go kill some old buffalos, set up the cooking pots. We will boil some then dry the rest. Skunk can have the horns to make his bows stronger, come let us go. The drying racks were ready water was boiling in the pots when the first hunters got back. Thirty skins were paged out and Skunk and his helpers tanned them. Every one worked on the meat the pots were filled and then meat was cut then on the racks to dry. Buffalo beef could be stored for winter or longer traded for anything, and when dry would keep a very long time you want some put it in water boil it. It was soft again.

By the time the meat was worked, more hunters were coming from another heard, with more bull buffalos on drag poles the forty two skins were paged out. Skunk got them ready for tanning. Between eating and storing of the dry meat, the process started over again.

Moon Boy and the pack full as ticks, slipped off to see his colt, eagle came too. Moon Boy talked to him, rubbed him and rested part of his weight on the colt broad back, and you need a name. I will call you, Golden Star and they will know of you far an near as eagle horse one who fly over land, like cloud shadows on a windy sun, you will have eyes on your feet and you will see badger holes, and never step in them, like my clay bank mare did. Then I never worry about sleeping forever, because you found that bad hole, and fell in it. We will find adventure together, you and me. But first we must grow you and me. You are too young to carry me far, even close but that will change soon. Golden stare we will fly over the land as one.

Eagle asked the stallion if he could give the boy a ride on his back, I think he would like that, only maybe not so fast in the turns, he rides well the bay is fast the bay is my grand son. I thought so eagle said. Does the bay know? I don't know it would make little difference. I think many of your horses from the crow are by me in one way or the other. We don't follow blood lines like they do. Bronze One the stallion that beat me is my grand son, and knew it but wanted my herd any way, I taught him how to win and he used that to beat me that is why I wanted to leave. Here the white stallion and the black stallion are both of my blood, but will not fight me, because they have nothing to gain. Yes I will give the little brave a ride, he is light I will not even feel him but you all come along just in case. Curly told Moon Boy to get on his back, he is so tall.

The stallion went to a drop made by water and stood Moon Boy got on his back. Moon Boy saw he could guide him with knee, so he rode to camp to brag a little all saw him good, he went to his lodge asked for his bow and quiver his mother handed them to him. She patted the horse. My, she said, and smiled. He saw Skunk tanning buffalo skins. Ho Skunk said, I see you are riding the wind he is the fast one, I have never seen one faster he likes you other wise you would never get near him. How is the work coming good but I have worked enough skins for one sun, I think I will look west and see, then I will help you.

Moon Boy went west past the old camp up the ridge and over to a place that lead to mule deer draw, here he turned north, then east and back to camp he stopped near Skunk still working on skins got off the stallion thanked him and turned to help Skunk. Skunk was about done with this bunch of skins. We have much meat made of old bull buffalo I think.

Moon Boy said. Yes and all as tough as a ash pole to, I hope we trade most of it, to the growers they can break their teeth on it, but it will get soft when boiled it will still be tough, even with spices it will not be as good as cow buffalo but we can eat it and will. And we still need thirty more from old bull buffalo, and then I am not sure that's enough. Let us see if any bull buffalo is still in the pots, I could eat now. Some was left so they did and yes it was as tough as ash trees but it was good to eat. Skunk had eaten it all his life, so was used to it. Next sun the hunters went for the last thirty bulls, Skunk said get me some young cows, I think I am hungry for buffalo but NOT old bull buffalo, all smiled that Skunk, he got to the meat of it, every time.

Moon Boy, Skunk and others went to look at the crops the bay as usual wanted to run he side stepped, pranced, even crow hopped a little but lined out, still wanting to run he had his grandfathers blood and it showed. I wonder if Golden Star will be like him in speed I hope in disposition I hope better. You see if you had to go quick, and he did not feel like it he would just stand there, and if you made him mad he would buck you down and kill you. He has a wild streak in him, that only love can concur and I think he is too old for that. But he is the greatest horse I have ever seen, or hope to see. At the fields they got of the horses and looked.

Chapter Twelve

Green vegetables were showing, pumpkins and squash little water melons to. The beans were blooming and the corn was showing tassels at the tops and tall. Soon silks would show, then ears, on the ears would be corn rows of golden, red and blue in color, the seed was called kernels food fit for man or beast. Skunk bent over to pull a weed and grandfather real snake began to sing, Skunk saw him and pulled the weed anyway. We must have the pack find them so some one don't get bit the field must worked soon, weeds are big. The hunters were coming with the buffalo, time to work skins thirty of them old bull buffalo and three young cows. Pots were made ready; Skunk and his helpers got the cow beef in the pots the water was boiling. When the meat was ready the rest would go in. Tall Elk asked braves to take forked stick and get the big snakes out of the fields, then he and the rest not needed in meat or skins went to the fields to weed, the entire band was working, the only way it could work. One for all and all for one!

They had the best fields, the best workers, the best horses and their scouts were unheard of before. Only this band of Sioux could brag of ground surveillance, air supremacy and over all control, of their destiny. They could lift their thumbs sky ward and say number one, and mean it. By late sun clouds could be seen forming, the weeds had once more been defeated and were gone from the crops.

Eleven big snakes had been removed, but most likely had returned to their leafy shelters. The Sioux did not kill them. They lived around them. True they did not want them in camp, and no they did not want them in the lodge or in their sleeping robes but they did help keep down the mice. And Skunk put their poison on arrow points, so you might say they played a part of life in and around the Sioux life. Kind of like a bad mother-in law. You maybe did not like her all time, but you did not kill her either.

Framework was done on the big lodge. Skunk and his helpers, and the women were lashing the cover together so they could put it up and tie it in place. One hundred bull buffalo skins were going to be heavy to lift. So they would go up in parts, the first section was going up now ten big braves were pushing and pulling. They lashed it at the opening and went around making it solid, it was cut so it would overlap on the top. The second section was in place. They lifted it and put it were it would be, then put it together, lashing every hole tight so it fit snug, then to the poles. The third section lay on the ground, getting the final adjustments to being hoisted up. Now they were ready up it came, and fit like a glove it to be lashed and tied in place, the smoke hole was fixed.

Moon Boy and his bunch were asked to bring sand in robes. Four boys to a robe and put a foot or more all the way around the big lodge they were almost finished, Skunk wanted to keep out mice and snakes they ate seeds, also it kept out the wind and water. Skunk tamped it with a pole and in some places it filled low spots, he asked for more new sand packers; get us more sand, they did. Tall Elk said we need a fire pit, so round smooth rocks were brought to make a pit the door was put up and shut. It was dark inside, good it is done now. Light a fire to see if the smoke hole works, a fire was kindled, flames shot up and the lodge was lighted up. It was big inside and the smoke curled out the hole.

Chapter Thirteen

Skunk sat down by the fire, Tall Elk joined him, bring in the bull buffalo and hang it. They did it took a long time most was put on the ground and piled up. Only the beef not full dry was hung. Skunk asked for four robes, two were spread out get my new bows and lay them on the robes. When it was done they made a pile, now cover them, they did. No one noticed it but it had clouded up. Thunder sounded, rain was falling. Slow at first then heavy. The new lodge sounded like a drum, it rained for a long time hard, and then settled to a mist. It would thunder and then the rain got heaver. Tall Elk said. "Good the grounds were getting hard and dry in some places in the crops. It was good we weeded them." When sun came, it was wet. All but the new lodge, it was dry as if no rain had fallen.

Good we have learned something, put sand around our lodges this yellow leaf time and we will be warmer when snow comes. Moon Boy, Skunk, Tall Elk, and Yellow Footed Dog, rode to see the crops. They were beautiful to look at; green leafs all sparkly with rain drops. The corn had grown a foot with silks showing now. The pumpkins five sun past were like round rocks. They were like boulders; the squash had grown also, but were shaped differently. The bean flowers were now pods with little beans in the pods. And the melons no one knew what they looked like, but they were getting bigger too.

Tall Elk asked Skunk, is our crop lodge big enough? I hope so, I would not like to think of eating more bull buffalo, and I hope the growers like them. Braves were working with the horses. Also the gelding the lesser stallions one year old or so they would be useful to the band as mounts and pack horses. There were too many studs and somebody would get killed.

The moon of roses had passed and so had the moon dry winds. It was the end of hot moon and the crop was ready to be brought in. No one thought they would have so many pumpkins and squash, the beans and corn that would need to dry on the plant more. They had eaten melons and learned to pick the ones with red centers. They were sweet and good but would not keep, and they saved as many seeds as they wanted drying them on robes, turning them often. Then put them in bags and hung them in the lodge for keeping. The pumpkins they cut in four took the seeds out of pulp and dried them, as they did the melons, and the pumpkins. They put holes to run lacings though and hung them to dry in the lodge, they did the same with the squash. Beans were dry in the pods; they were hard so the band thought maybe better get them in before it got wet again.

Now how to do it, four people to a row, two on each side pick bean pods, putting them in a bag. Take bags to camp were others shelled them and put them in still other bags to hang.

Five suns later the beans were in, and what a sight it was bull buffalo they moved to every ones lodges to store, to make room for the crop. Corn was a problem, deer, porcupine, coons' even skunks wanted it, and so they picked it. Long ears of corn, they took just the ears to camp leaving all else in the field. The corn was golden, red, white blue and other colors all mixed up together. It was shelled on robes as not to let any get lost then bagged and hung, seed corn first. Then for eating the lodge was full. A fire was kept burning so it could stay dry.

Tall Elk, Skunk, and other band leaders came to the crop lodge just to sit and look. They found the cobs burned well so they were used it for fuel. Skunk sat and thought long before he spoke. Our band of Sioux this season has done much more then others of our kind has ever done. Moon Boy, and our spirit guides and eagles have made this happen; the pack saved us by warning us when the crow came first. And again when they came, then they went on guard to keep us safe.

Eagle flew to watch; eagle brought us the golden stallion, and saved Moon Boys life by getting the pack in time. Then we grow a crop, and have more food, more then any of our kind ever had. We have a strong chief. He showed us how to work together to get things done and I Skunk say thank you. I have spoken! No one said anything. Then a cheer went up that you could have heard for miles.

Moon Boy and the pack came and sat. Some times it is good to sit with friends, and say nothing. Tall Elk cleared his wind pipes, and said. "You arrow makers, make some arrows a little longer to fit Skunks new bows better. Some we will use others we can trade. I hope we have no war but it is good to be ready."

Moon Boy, ask if eagle is near. If she is I would talk with her. Every one looked up expecting eagle to be there, and then she was. Tall Elk said. "Eagle I have a feeling all is not well. I think the enemies are watching us would you go look? Yes I will and was gone.

Eagle was back, two young braves are looking at the horses they try to steal mounts they have none. Some of you go get them and bring them here, Moon Boy take the pack and go to. Skunk soon we go to the growers to exchange some of what we have for things we have not. What do we need? Skunk said. "I have heard of a plant, the crop grows in the ground. It is called "pot-a-toes" potatoes. I would like to try to grow them we need more cooking pots to, and more long knifes and tomatoes seeds, and if they have pepper seed them to, and what ever we can use.

Moon Boy and the others, and the pack brought in the two braves. Why were you in our horse herd? They were after the golden stallion, Moon Boy said. Tall Elk laughed, "The more I wonder why you are not dead." He is with us because he wants to be, we could never hold him if he wanted to go. What are you called, and where are you from? We are Mandan's from the big river country. Are you from Blue Corns band? Yes do you know him? Of course we go to see him soon we will trade with him some of what we have, for what he has. You are lucky we kill horse thieves, but you will be returned to Blue Corn unharmed I will trade you for something. You will be our gests until we go, if you try to go first I will tie you to the post.

That is not a pleasant thing to happen. Our spirit guides, the wolf pack will watch you if you try to get away, they will bring you back, no one can get far when they watch. We go in six or seven suns you will go then and answer to Blue Corn for trying to steel horses from us. The golden stallion yet, I am wondering why you are not all over the prairie in many small pieces. He doesn't like strangers so you were lucky again.

The store lodge was full. The people were eating the pumpkin and squash that did not fit, there was still many of them to bring in. You can help, my son and some of his band will work with you, bring them all. Now what do they call you? I am called Fox Tail and I am Frogs Foot, Tall Elk asked. "Where are your sleeping robes? And where are your horses?" Our horses got free, with our robes on them. That is why we tried to get horses to catch ours." Tall Elk and Skunk looked long at each other. Skunk shook his head, Moon Boy ask eagle if she saw two horses with robes on, no just the two of them. Eagle saw no horses with you, why are you not telling the truth? Now sit down and tell it true or you get the post. I will tell the truth, you were stealing horses and got caught, and you may not have known. This is Tall Elks band of Sioux and that we trade with Blue Corn, but you were steeling horses and we should kill you for it. Do you want to die? No we don't THEN TELL TRUE, or die.

Fox Tail was scared we are growers sons. We want to be warriors or braves we don't want to grow. We have no horse or bow or any arrows no club or ax, so we came to steel from the Sioux. We knew you have all; Skunk and Tall Elk exchanged looks. You also have no robes, no food, no lodge and no people how are you going to be braves? Skunk said. "One more thing you don't have is brains. I think we should kill you and save some one the pain of it." Tall Elk said, "We could show you dead warriors out on the prairie, who were better then you by far, but are dead because they tried to fight us. Tie them to the post, you will stand there for two suns, you are going back to Blue Corn we can't use you we don't need babies. But think when you are standing. If your people take you back eagle did not fly the first sun, and the pack did not kill game the first try, and you almost got killed trying to steel the golden stallion, two times. Now tie them."

"Moon Boy asks someone to help get the rest of the crop in, use drags put them by the lodge were all can get them. We will get the goods to trade ready go. We will take thirty five braves and twenty five or so pack horses, when we get close we will kill some good buffalo for them, as part of the trade. We will trade the two at the post to, but we will not get much for them." I Tall Elk will go mounted on the white stallion. Moon Boy will go with ten of his braves, One Skunk, Looking Back Horse, Looking Eagle, Horse Dung, Yellow Footed Dog, The Skunk You Can Not See, Spotted Owl, Runs Fast, Bulls Tail, Stands Tall, Buffalo Tongue, Drinks Plenty, Brings Horse, Circle Eagle, Hawk Thunder, Goes First, Prairie Dog, Last Horse, Wind In His Hair, Eagles Tail, Antelope Horn, Deer Legs, Fast Duck and Comes Back will go on the trade for things we need Iron People will be chief when we are gone, with Taken Alive, the two will watch the band.

The pack will go and one eagle or two eagles will watch to see no body bothers our camp. We will take the lesser bows and some arrows, robes and the bags. We brought seeds in some arrow points a few knifes a couple of lances half of old bull buffalo dried meat. Someone take food and water for the two at the post but leave them tied. Moon Boy got all the crops in by now and it made quite a pile. The braves going get your horses up get good bows and fill your quivers with arrows. We may go early. Moon Boy get your bay and ask the spirit guides to be ready. Eagle, get up thirty pack horses and let's start packing. Skunk choose the bows we can do with out and some lesser arrows. Always keep the best for us.

Old bull buffalo was hard to pack. It was bulky and heavy and took more horses to transport then one would think, but it was loaded along with the rest. Get the two at the post, they wanted to ride horse now they can, there legs would not hold them at first, get mounted or we will drag you, or we can put you over them and you can ride head down, they got mounted. Tall Elk waved his arm and they were in motion. A long line of horse men thundered over the prairie. Tall Elk dropped back to see how the packs were riding, he rode beside Looking Back Horse and Buffalo Tongue for a time, then back to the end to look at Blue Corns two they were bouncing along. Looking like they wished they were some place, any place then were they were at.

Do you like to ride horse? No they said, "We will grow beans, but I thought you would be warriors or braves they do this most every sun. Maybe now you will be better growers, and I won't have to kill you so often. Next time, you come calling see me first or your bones may bleach on the prairie. They were out on the flats way north of the Moreau River now moving well at a ground eating rolling lope.

It was September now and the air warm and sweet birds were flocking and getting ready to go south. The grass was golden and yellow with green mixed though out. All the grass eaters were fat and lazy, laying in groups or standing just enjoying life. There was some water in the stream so they watered the horses, went across and rode on. Horses were lathered but that was good, the Grand River brakes were shimmering under the sun. It was so fine it made one want to break out in a song.

Skunk did but he carried his bow better then a tune. Curly tried covering his ears, but it was hard to run and cover the sound, so he howled a little and ran on. They splashed across the Grande then up on the rolling flat land turning north east, making good time. Some of the older and lesser horses were showing stress so they walked for a little. Some of the braves walked to, letting the mounts rest and cool they mounted and moving again at a swinging lope a gate, they went though miles like a group of boys eat soup on a cool sun. Long shadows danced in front of them pointing east, game were every place one looked. They found the spring and made camp, killed a young dry buffalo cow, got fires going and had hump ribs sizzling before it could be spoke of all ate his fill.

Then talked a bit then were sleeping, the wolves on guard except Curly who snored on Moon Boys right and Cubby on his left. At first light, meat was cooking, Sioux style. That means wipe its nose and butt and bring it. Just slightly singed, but well if you like it that way, I like it cooked a little more.

When sun was turning the east pink they were riding, all that was left at the spring was bones and meat, and very little of that. Skunk took the hide he tanned it last night, to good to leave. The horses left their piles of used grass and the braves left piles of used meat. I am going to tell you something I found out, we come, we stay a little, we go and we leave very little in our passing. (I leave this book to you; it is my thoughts on how it could have been and maybe was.)

Tall Elk took them east at a long lope the horses had rested and were fresh and the sound that came out from under all those hooves is something I will never forget. Sun was half way to mid sun when the brakes of the big river came in sight. It was the second time he had seen it, but it still made him stop and look. He took them of the hill to the grower's camp.

Blue Corn was there. Welcome my friend, and how was your year? Good we grew much crop. We brought much dry buffalo meat, some bows and arrows, robes some lances and a little more. We also have two of yours that tried to steal from us. I have brought them back to you. We should have killed them and if they come again we will. "Bring them". The two stood in front of Blue Corn, who looked long at them. Go to your lodges I will speak to you later. Tall Elk asked, "Do you need meat? We could kill buffalo for you". Yes we could use ten or so get pole drags and get ten or so, it was done. Unload the dry meat, the bows and arrows. Blue Corn asked what you need. Cooking pots, dry peppers and seed potatoes, may be some long knifes and the salt. How do we keep the potatoes, they must not freeze, dig a hole in a bank by your river ten feet in and six feet over put them in and cover the opening with six foot of soil leave them there until you plant. Come in the spring we will show you how to plant peppers. Now we eat and they did large platters of good food, steaming bowls of some thing but good to. Now it was the cooking pots.

Skunk loved the pots and as usual they had all his favorite, so if he was first to get at the pots to bad, if he could have got ten bowls in his hands he would have ten bowls. But the meal was over, and every one just rested. No one felt like starting back on full stomach or loading a lot of things that would have to be Skunk asked to see the tools they used in growing crops and when he saw them, they were no better then the ones he had contrived maybe not as good that made him feel good.

Skunk was pretty good when it came to building something, with just an idea of how it should look. Tall Elk asked, "How they watered the paints, if it was dry this growing season they had not needed to, it rained when they needed it." Blue Corn said, "You need fifty water jugs then fill them and form a line and just carry them to the plants change of often so no person gets to tired. I will make you some this snow time. Then when you come to see how we plant peppers, you can take them. I will send some tomatoes seeds to. You must start them in your lodges. In the flats and then you set them out when frost is past. You will like them. It makes good in cooking pots or eat them when they get red. Good for you to."

When sun was new they got the pack horses and loaded the things they had traded for. Skunk saw to loading of the pots, he did not want one broken five horses would carry the seed potatoes, two horses would carry the other seeds, five horses would carry corn seed a new kind, six horses would carry long knives and all the rest they had traded for including honey. The other pack horses could just run, until they got to the grand then Skunk would get bow wood he liked to make bows and arrows. All were mounted. The pack ready and eagle also. So they waved and started out. Over the long hill and out on the flats at a long easy lope, they watered at the spring and rode on. Still at the long easy lope, now to a spanking trot then to a walk. Let them blow some.

It was past middle sun when they got to the grand. Skunk and Moon Boy and his braves got bow wood. Skunk wanted to be prepared so they killed a young bull. The hump ribs were cooking. The horses grazed and rested. Tall Elk sat down by Skunk. You should get more bow wood this is not nearly enough, and we could get more if we camp now. In the next sun we could all look for bow wood. The horses are tired so let us camp, eat more buffalo and then we will see. All ate more.

Skunk tried to clean his ear it must be plugged and he thought some one said get bow wood Skunk. One Skunk was a wonderful human being, every body loved him, he was a friend to all, he would do most anything for any body he was never cross or ill tempered. But he worked hard, he sweat a lot, and washed little so if he took of his foot ware, every body down wind just moved up wind and could be heard to say Skunk is named well he smells just like a skunk and that was not bad it was more a compliment then anything. So they made camp, ate more buffalo talked some, smoked a little got their robes, and slept.

At sun up they ate more buffalo and all helped Skunk get wood for bows. Now with so much help, they got the best only. At last Skunk said "we now have enough". With that, they loaded the packs and started for camp.

The horses were rested and moved out well, at a rolling lope. It was cool so the pace got faster they were going to home camp and knew it. The ground was flying past, so Tall Elk pulled in some and brought them down to a gait. They could keep for a long ways. They come to the little stream, crossed it and went on not breaking stride. Now the Moreau River breaks were in sight. On a long ridge they stopped the horses to blow. They were covered with sweat and foam, sides heaving. "Let them cool of some". They started again walking them. Then at a slow canter not forcing them, dropping of the ridge into the Moreau River country. Then up to the camp.

Skunk's son June Bug around ten summers asked his father, "father did you see any little girls"? Before Skunk could say a word, Looking Back Horse said, no June Bug he was to busy, looking at the big little girls. Skunk hung his head, then glanced at Looking Back Horse, who was grinning from ear to ear, they all were. Skunk's wife Rose Bud said she would go along next time. The pant stud could carry two. Then I can keep my eye on him better. Yellow Footed Dog you and Spotted Owl pick five braves each, and then go fined a place to dig a potato cave. We need it to be six feet over the top, and big enough to put our potato seed in, deep enough so it won't freeze, take long knives and sharpen poles to dig with. Find a bank tall enough so the water can't get in, and then mark it so we can find it again. Thirty of you go take out all the old plaints out of our fields, put to one side to be feed to our horses in deep snow time.

The rest help unload the packs. They had ten of so cooking pots. Skunk took one of the smaller pots for himself; the rest was put in the storage lodge. The sacks of new corn seed were hung high up in the big lodge, so was the pepper and tomato seeds, then all the rest. Now the storage lodge was full, not much more would fit. So Tall Elk, Skunk, Moon Boy and others whet to see how the cave diggers were doing. When they got there, they found a hole in the bank well started,

Curly and Cubby jumped in this was right down their alley, the dirt flew out of the hole, and when they got tired two more jumped in and no one told them to they just did. Tall Elk said the pack got the job. They will dig back to the camp and turn around and be back before long. Moon Boy said, "Stop let us see how far you are." Yellow Footed Dog crawled in to look, he came out with a round white some thing a skull, Ho how did it get here? An old one in the long ago got caught in the mud, and was covered with more mud now he is out. Go in and dig a place to put our seeds in.

Two went in then the wolves dug the dirt out Skunk went in and came out with some yellow gravely some thing that glistened in the sun he sat down and looked at it he turned it in his hands. I think this will cause a lot of trouble some sun. There are skin sacks in there with this in them I will take this back. Go to camp and bring some bags the old ones are no good, we will see.

Tall Elk was back with bags Skunk very carefully put the Gold in new leather bags, four bags in all. Under the skin sacks was a strange head piece Skunk brought it out, when it was brushed of it was shinny silver white in color and hard. It had a red stone set in its center that shot red fire when the sun caught it. Skunk went back in dug more and found three knives all made of the hard silver something, one as long as big braves leg and curved up at the end. The long knife had a handle and grip. The grip had the yellow gold some thing on it was hard, shinny and beautiful to see. Skunk grabbed the handle and swung the blade. It whistled as it cut the air. Skunk knew he had something in his hand made to kill braves with. You could cut someone in to with one swing. We will take the knives and leave the head thing and gold in the cave. We will make a hole to one side and cover them again, but first let me go look to make sure we have it all.

Skunk went back in and dug around, finding a something to put on your finger. He knew that it was on a finger. Skunk came out and showed the ring. It was made of the gold, and had a stone of red fire on it, all cut and polished with red fire gleaming from it, we will put it away to, it will draw to much attention if seen, they will want to know how we got it. Let us go in and smooth the bottom, then lay buffalo skins to put potato on. In doing one more bag came up, it held round pieces of gold, with pictures on them. Skunk showed them to all, an opening was made to one side, and their treasure was put in a robe and reburied. A rock was pushed in, then dirt. Now bring in the seed, the potato seed was spread out, then a robe more seed, until all seed was in then a robe. Get rocks they covered the back of the opening, now dirt pack it, more rocks then dirt, rocks they finished with soil, smoothed it down marked it so they could find it again. No one would guess a fortune in gold and gems were with the seed potato.

Tall Elk and Skunk rode in front on the way back to camp. They turned around and spoke to the rest. We do not know what the gold is worth, but if found out I am sure. Someone would come from over the big waters to get it. They would kill us all or try to. Just to have it so say nothing not even to your wife. It is safe as long as we tell no one, Moon Boy, no one is to know. I feel some sun others will come to our prairies not like the Sioux, or crow but different from us. The one we found who had the treasure was not from here. He came from some place, but where? And why was he by himself. If some one finds out from one of us the blood of all will be on him. The long knifes made of the shinny hard thing, we will say we found at the growers that will be enough, and they have many things we do not have. Say nothing about the rest.

"Skunk, make a very good bow out of that wood we have. Use all your tricks I will watch". I would see you do this. Some of you should work the young horses before snow time gets here. Others get some meat put water on beans and corn we will eat well to say thank you for a safe trip just past. Skunk I will watch you do this thing now, we will see. Skunk was proud to work on a bow, for his chief he went to his bow wood pile and got a piece of oak, his best. Come Tall Elk and sit, watch and learn. He took the long slender wood and held it in his hands, getting its spirit, its feel and balance. When he found the balance he shaved of slivers of wood, it must be as slender at one end as the other, or it would not snap, and have less power.

Skunk had some rough rock, this he used to smooth down the bow; he bent the bow over his knee testing it for power it must send the shaft very fast to be any good. He had cut, shaved and smoothed the wood, it was thick in the middle, going to slender out to the ends, here he cut it, then notched it. Skunk closed his eyes running the bow back and forth in his hands, and then he got horn shell and laid it on the bow, all the time his glue was getting hot on the fire. Now he smeared glue on the middle part of the bow. Skunk then put horn shell on pressing them down hard, more glue overlapping the pieces all the way around now down the back side of the bow. He went past mid point on two sides, then back again to middle bow and did it again, always overlapping and smoothing the strips down.

He put more wood on the fire, slowly passing the bow over the flames cooking the horn and glue as one. Skunk did this many times, until most of the bow was all most ridged, most of the bend at the ends were the snap and the power was. His glue was made of boiled hooves of buffalo and horse, some plant and other things I can't say, Skunks secret, but very sticky, they fletched arrows with this same glue. Skunk put the bow to one side to cool and harden. Then took a sheet of raw hide that had been soaking for a long time, this Skunk very carefully wrapped around and around the bow, and then tied it in place, so it could not move. It would dry and shrink and get smaller and tighter, holding the raw hide in place.

Skunk told Tall Elk let it lay flat for a few suns and get hard then try it. It should send an arrow very far and very fast. Thank you my brother and good friend I will use it proudly all my suns. All will know it is one of Skunks bows, and every one will want one like it. Yellow Footed Dog and The Skunk You Can Not See said Skunk I may need a new bow or ten do you have enough bow wood? Or should we get more, it never hurts to have plenty of wood on hand. One Skunk looked at them a long time, then said go then get more bow wood, get very small twigs for your bows I want you to be able to pull them, we don't want any mad mice looking for you two.

Moon Boy had been working with golden star. He did not weigh much and star was big so no one was too surprised to see Moon Boy come in on star with the now ever present wolf pack on all sides. Tall Elk and Skunk got up and came to run their hands over the big stud colt, my he is fine, and I never saw a better colt. Can he run? Yes, but not like the stallion he is young yet. Skunk said," When he is three he will be faster, I think. Don't ride him much you could hurt him, take him back and ride one of the other horses back. Yes bring horses for me and Skunk I would try my bow and have some meat to."

Moon Boy rode the colt back to the horse herd, found the bay and switched horses. He got the white stallion and Skunks pinto stud and went to camp. Yellow Footed Dog said he would go to, as did Horse Dung and Runs Fast old Iron People said he had not pounded his but horse back in some time, so he would go. Looking Back Horse said if I let you out of my sight for more then fart or two, you will fall off a cliff and eat dirt or something so I had better go too.

It was fall now the nights were cool, before they got going ten or so others had got bows, horses and pack horses. "Elk then?" Yes let's go get elk. Skunk smiled and licked his lips, good it was good. Tall Elk led on the white stallion, Skunk rode beside him on his pinto stud, Moon Boy rode to the left on his bay with white fore legs, Curly on his right, and Cubby on his left. The she wolf, Fatty, and Dusty Rose, in front. The rest of the pack fanned out behind. Nothing was going to bother Moon Boy as long the pack was near.

We don't always smell the same. When it is hot our sweat smells one way. If we hear a snake rattle real close, but we can't see him fear makes us smell different again. If we stumble over something and it sounds like shells clinking together we smell like fear and our sweat is different from all the rest. Grandfather snake knows the smell of fear. The pack knew all of Moon Boys smells and they were ever on guard to his well being, he could not see well but they did.

Even in his handy cap he was ten times safer then anyone else. The bay knew this to, he never placed his feet wrong or he would have to answer to the pack and his mother never had any dumb colts, and if that was not enough they could talk to each other, even at high speeds, such a team was never formed before and never will be again.

I am giving you a look inside their heads at a near prefect world, where there were no orphans, no widows, no one on the edge of starvation no one was paid, you did your turn when you could and it was a rule all lived by. Eagle would fly in the direction of their course when it was clear to her; he would come back and report as to what was ahead. This sun they were hunting game not enemies that was clear. Big groups of buffalos grazed undisturbed any way you looked. Flocks of antelopes showed their white rumps as they raced up on a ridge, only to turn and stand and look, as the horse men pasted by. Iron People rode by Skunk, I had to come up beside you old friend, my horse was chocking, he likes air that smells good not air just passed over you, you should go fall in a river, a very big river. Skunk said, you were ridding backwards again? You were smelling yourself. Moon Boy and the pack snickered, that Skunk could tell them. Tall Elk told them all, the Skunk smells good, he can smell a Prairie Dog fart up to two miles Ho, that's too far said Looking Back Horse, that's what I say Skunk smells good. Laughter sounded up and down the line even Skunk smiled then laughed too. Skunk said when we get to the river I will wash one foot. Why not wash all over Horse Dung said, then we could eat fish for a week, they would be coming up like wood down stream, we could even smoke them, it will not work I can never keep them lit. All laughed again! Every body loved Skunk, he was funny and a better friend could not be found anywhere. When they reached the river Skunk rode his stud in the, water belly deep, and slid of, after leaving his bow and quiver with Tall Elk. Get behind your ears Skunk some one ran down stream and found a dead fish and through it to the swimmer, see they are up already now we can eat fish, you eat fish I will eat elk. Skunk came out of the water shook water off and went to the fire to dry and soon he was.

Tall Elk killed a buffalo cow with one arrow, at quite a distance this bow he told Skunk is the best I ever had I thank you again my friend, but it is not elk. We will camp then we will find elk, and cook them in pots. Good said Skunk. Fires were made bigger soon hump ribs were sizzling and other meat was cooking over the open flames it was good.

Skunk tanned the skin, putting it meat side down then put his robe on top, and covered with them and was sleeping, still cold from getting wet long before the others. Eagle got part of the heart, and some strips of meat Tall Elk cut for her, the pack had their fill to, and raw is how they liked it. Curly and the rest of the pack were on guard duty.

Grand father bear was said to be in this place from time to time and if the she wolf was right you just got out of his way, he had a bad temper, and very big. The pack split to cover more ground, soon Curly and Cubby would go to be with Moon Boy, big snake was here also, if you rolled on him he would give you his poison, and kill you maybe. They found him to close to Moon Boy, Curly got him behind his head, and Cubby bit him in his coils and tore him in two, should we eat him? You can, he give me gas.

Skunk was up getting cooking fires going, he found the snake tore in two he looked at Moon Boy bed with the wolves sleeping with him, he shook his head, when you have loyal friends like that, you were rich beyond belief, friends like that were better then gold, or a women favors but Moon Boy was to young to know that, or the wolves either.

Responsibilities came with that, baby on the floor getting in to your bow making equipment cutting his finger on an arrow point then making enough sound to bring on a uprising, then the wife screaming at you to be more careful with your dumb old war stuff or she would go to mothers, and when you said as nice as you can, don't forget to take baby she got your war club and ran you out of the lodge with it. Or when you got back from a long ride getting enough food to last a few suns, she had all of her relatives over and they ate the entire trip again, then she would say very nice. Skunk we will need more meat very soon, you are to big to cry so you get a fresh horse and go hunting again, bone tired and mad enough to eat a grand father real snake tail first. Skunk had been there, in all the above, but now he wanted to hunt elk for the cooking pots, and the skins.

He got Moon Boy up he wanted the boy along to scout with him. They got their horses and went to look, no elk close, they rode up river quite a ways before they found elk not the main herd, but a few. Some bulls two or three of them, cows and some spike bulls, calves and old animals to. They were in a bend of the river in and out of the cotton woods browsing on brush and downed leaves. Skunk signed to get the others, Moon Boy wormed to the horses got his bay and he with the pack went to get the others, Skunk is up river watching the elk, he is waiting for us lets go. All said Ho lets go kill elk, so they did, Tall Elk got two one of the large bulls and a spike bull, Skunk killed a fat dry cow two more went down. Iron People killed a spike bull and Looking Back Horse an old bull with lance horns. All helped in the getting ready to go.

Eagle got half of a heart, the pack got theirs not much liver preferred by some of the braves, let us go cook elk, so they did. The cooking pots were full of water, beans and corn was soaking. A scout was watching from a ridge as soon as they were seen fires were lighted under the pots when they got there steam was just started to rise of the water. Skunk started cutting meat almost before all had stopped moving. Elk meat was good very good. The entire band liked it better then other meat. The elk feast went as planed Skunk being the first to fill his dish, and the last to say enough, all over ate, and no one was hungry the next sun or some the one after that.

The horse heard had grown long hair, for winter protection, so had the pack and dogs of the people. Most of the buffalo had drifted south, some had stayed, and they never all went south. It was mid November, and getting cold at night. But that was alright all the prairie folk were ready, it was the way of things. The wolves would winter far better then the she wolf had for they had the Sioux band and the band would be better off because of the pack.

All knew better then to bother Tall Elks Sioux by now, if you wanted to keep a whole hide, that is. Between the pack on the ground and eagles in the sky no one could get through at all, most did not understand it, but all knew it. The big lodge of one hundred bull buffalo skins was full of food and seeds for the new growing season.

The young boys and girls had made a game of heaping sand around the outside until it was almost air tight. Also a fire was kept inside burning, a little fire but it kept the damp out. Someone was grinding corn most of the time; corn meal had become a staple of the people. Tall Elk was a good chief and a lucky one, no one had gotten sick and most were hardy, and well fed. But there was sadness to, old buffalo women had crossed over, there was others resting in trees too, that was to be expected no one lived forever. Only the rocks and land lived on. Doves Tail, Tall Elks second wife was showing child and would be born in the moon of long night's just two moons away. There were others in the band to have baby also, life goes on you come, you go then new life is here.

Curly and the wolf pack had been digging a new den just up the draw from the old den much larger and hidden better it was in a buffalo berry patch, half way up a steep hill. All the dirt would be gone the first big rain in the spring. Moon Boy had brought old robes for beds and much grass and leaves; they fixed up the first den to with robes and other things not needed by the people. Others of the pack may want to mate as well, but would stay together as long as food was enough and that looked good.

In mid December it snowed much snow, and then a blast of cold air from the North West brought a blizzard that lasted three suns. Braves moved the horse herd to deep draws well grassed but two old horses had not made it, their teeth was bad, so the pack ate them, and eagles too. Nothing was just left, someone or something always made use of it. Jack rabbits were in good numbers to, so the pack would spook them up and eagle would kill them, all ate well. By this time more old horses had died so they ate them to.

Big cat had to be run off a few times, he liked his horse meat warm, this could not be. One time the pack kept him in a tree for two suns dripping blood from many cuts and slashes and when they let him go he went. He looked back and screamed, I will be back a bad thing to say this time he had to set in a bad tree, three suns new blood dripping, he was nice after that he just was gone. Mess with the bull; you get the horn every time. He liked rabbit much better now.

January was ten suns old, when Tall Elk had a new son in his lodge. Dove Tail had gave him a little boy baby, it had been hard; he did not want to come out. He liked it nice and warm but in the end he was born. Curly and Blue Dawn had taken to hunting at night, running the long ridges playing in the snow, dashing though the meadows sliding on the ice but finding little food.

Now, after a week or so, things at the new den were back to normal. The she wolf would sit and looked wise and explained the law, as she had when the pups were little. Fatty and Ling Lang were nervous, they had no feelings to mate, but Curly had, and he did. Mother explained some male wolves did not mate until two or three years old, or until ready. Curly was first born and she was alone, so he had responsibilities you never had, he grew up fast. He had to his time clock moved up a notch so now he will be a father first it is part of the law we must live by. But it will be better now we will all help with the young, and food will be more with the band to help and Moon Boy will be aloud to come and help but no one else, not for awhile anyway.

I may mate again and I may not, that big lobo calls to me at night, but he is not a father figure. I think he will be gone just when I need him most and I don't want to go though that again, you were enough, and I was lucky to get you all big and not have any of you die. If I let old cruel fangs come, he will want to fight Curly for leader ship, then we would kill him, and I don't want him to hurt Moon Boy or the band of man things we protect. So I think I will not do that thing, I will wait. Curly, Cubby, Fatty and Sniff lopped over to camp to see Tall Elks new baby boy, can he see? Was the question they asked? We hope so Doves Tail said, it is too early to say. Curly said some of my pups will help him grow up as I and Cubby helped Moon Boy, so he will be safe from harm, she smiled, and said then he will be blessed, as Moon Boy is. Thank you.

Chapter Fourteen

Time moved along, as it moves now more babies was born, more people were in trees waiting for the last sun rise to come, so they could go home. It was past mid March when the pups came, five of them three males and two little she wolves. Blue Dawn had been told through instinct that down though history, that father had to be watched or they would kill the young, but there sat Curly watching his offspring amazed and helpful in every way, and Cubby lay at full length, his chin on his paws looking on. Fatty and Ling Lang looked on to the rest mothered the young licking them and softly talking to them. Were they getting spoiled? Yes, you could say that, oh well grand mothers and aunts have been doing this in every race since the beginning of time, I am not surprised, are you?

Curly got Moon Boy who came on the high run to see, he brought food, it was not needed there was rabbits, prairie dogs, mice even a spring bird of some kind, all for Blue Dawn to eat when she went for water and to relieve herself. They argued to see who would keep them warm, who would lick them and change them, now I am getting carried away.

One spring sun, after the new crops were all in and growing, in front of Tall Elks lodge, Little Eagle Plum young son of Tall Elk was asleep resting on Curly's shoulder, his chubby little fingers holding on to the fur of two wolf cubs, who was all so sleeping. Cubby was there to as was Moon Boy. One Skunk and Tall Elk walked up softly as to not disturb the resting. Skunk looked at the sun and said, from where the sun stands now, then and will forever stand, I see a good life, for us all.

About the Author

My family's homestead was on the Moreau River country on the rolling plains of South Dakota. I was born in 1936 with a birth defect that gave me limited use of my arms and legs. However, I overcame many obstacles from shooting a gun to driving a car to painting pictures by mouth.

I went to grade school in a one room school house. Graduated from high school in Dupree SD and then went to SDSU, where I graduated with a Bachelor of Science degree in Art. I returned to my parent's ranch until I married in 1971. My wife, Faith and I, had three children: Katherine Francis, Melody Jane and Heather June. I enrolled in the Mouth and Foot Painting Artists. Which is an association were artists all over the world paint either by mouth or foot. Then in 2002, I lost my wife in a tragic vehicle accident that put me in a wheelchair.

The places I speak of in my book are real. I have been there. Some of the names are real, most I invented. If any person or persons' names are used in this book it would only be coincidental. I have let my mind run free and dreamed up a world as it should have been, could have been and maybe was. I have enjoyed writing this book and I hope you do too.

Printed in the United States
35581LVS00007B/250-279

9 781420 858921